M000029061

DEATH WILL COME AT DAWN

"Stilwell and his scouting party tell me they counted some six hundred lodge circles on the ground around us. That would mean something like twice that many warriors, wouldn't it, Sharp?"

"Thousand at least," Grover replied.

"Twenty of them to one of us," a scout said. "We're asking for real trouble, pushing them like this, aren't we, Major?"

In the deepening twilight, the men's faces were indistinct so that Forsyth could recognize only those in the front ranks —hard-bitten plainsmen like Donovan, Trudeau, and the older Farley; adventurers like Burke and Gantt; mere boys like Schlesinger, Stilwell, and the younger Farley. "Every man of you was told before enlisting what the mission of this scouting company would be," he said firmly. "Did you not enlist with me to fight Indians?"

"Aye, sir, we did that," declared Martin Burke. Someone else cried: "A thousand hostiles don't faze us, Major. If they're looking for a fight, we'll see they get one."

ACTION AT BEECHER ISLAND

Dee Brown

A DELL BOOK

ISBN: 0-440-20180-2

Printed in the United States of America

Published simultaneously in Canada

December 1988

10 9 8 7 6 5 4 3 2 1

KRI

Foreword

This story of the nine-day siege of Forsyth's Scouts by Plains Indians at Beecher Island in September 1868 is based upon reports, diaries, letters, and accounts of participants. Each man who experienced the ordeal at Beecher Island saw or remembered it in a different way; therefore it is presented here from the varying viewpoints of Lieutenant Frederick Beecher, Chief-of-Scouts Abner (Sharp) Grover, Major George Forsyth, Jack Stilwell, Sigmund Schlesinger, Martin Burke, Two Crows, Roman Nose, John Donovan, Reuben Waller, and Captain Louis Carpenter.

Interviews with surviving Indians, accounts of Scouts Thomas Ranahan, Eli Ziegler, Thomas Murphy, John Hurst, George Oakes, Chauncey Whitney, A. J. Pliley, Louis McLaughlin, James J. Peate, Chalmers Smith, and official records and reports of the War Department are supporting sources.

Whenever possible the dialogue—which is introduced for dramatic effect and to forward the action—is in words recorded by witnesses or participants.

1

Lieutenant
Frederick Beecher

May 1868

A gust of wind swept through the open door of the quartermaster's office, lifting papers from Lieutenant Frederick Beecher's battered desk. He patiently retrieved them from the floor, weighting them down with a piece of polished pink sandstone. The wind had brought with it an aroma of springtime, and when Beecher looked across the Fort Wallace parade ground to the sloping prairie beyond, he could see a shimmer of greening buffalo grass.

Anywhere else, he thought, spring was a welcome season, but around Fort Wallace it usually meant Indian troubles. The buffalo herds were moving north to graze, and hostile bands of Cheyennes and Sioux would soon be coming down from their winter camps to hunt. After the hunts would come the raiding parties—against settlers, ranchers, railroad construction crews, wagon trains and stagecoaches. Last summer Roman Nose had boldly challenged the fort itself, and only a valiant stand by a company of the 7th Cavalry had saved it from disaster.

Beecher was reaching for his quill pen when he heard footsteps pounding on the wooden sidewalk outside. As he glanced again toward the open door, the bulky form of the post's sergeant major almost filled the entrance. "Lieutenant Beecher, sir," the sergeant said. "General Sheridan requests your presence at headquarters."

Beecher stared hard at the sergeant major. "General Sheridan?"

"Yes, sir."

"I'll be right along, Sergeant." Beecher kicked off his ragged moccasins and searched under the desk for his black boots. He had not worn them for so long they were dusty. He cleaned them hurriedly, brushed his weather-stained forage cap, tightened his cravat and pushed it into the collar opening.

When he stepped out on the windy parade, he felt the accustomed twinge from his old knee wound, and then started limping toward the flagpole and headquarters. He wondered what "Little Phil" Sheridan could have to say to him, a mere lieutenant assigned to quartermaster duties at this lonely outpost.

General Sheridan had arrived on the stage last night from the railhead thirteen miles east, and everyone had been alert all day for an inspection, but none had been called. Perhaps this was Little Phil's way of running an inspection—summoning the various duty officers to make reports.

Beecher glanced off to the right, noting with satisfaction that his construction crew at work on a new commissary was making good progress. This was the third stone building he had supervised, and he was proud of their solid permanence, the pink-colored limestone walls in bright relief against the drab plateau. The generals back east might consider Fort Wallace a jumping-off place to nowhere, he thought, but if they leave me and my quartermaster crew alone for another year there won't be a better-built post west of the Missouri.

The generals back east . . . It had not been so long since General Sheridan was one of them, making history with that famous ride from Winchester down the Valley of Virginia.

> Up from the South, at break of day
> Bringing to Winchester fresh dismay . . .

Hurrah! hurrah for Sheridan!
Hurrah! hurrah for horse and man!

Beecher smiled to himself. Little Phil Sheridan. Beecher had heard someone say that Sheridan had been an Indian fighter out here in the West before the war, and was a good choice now to command the harassed Department of the Missouri. Time would tell. Remembering the scrap of poem made him remember the Civil War. He hadn't had much time for thinking of the past since he'd been out here in western Kansas. Three bad wounds he'd got in the war—thigh, foot, and knee, the last and worst at Gettysburg which took him out of action for good. But he'd come back into the Army, settling gladly for a quartermaster assignment that a lame man could easily handle.

His feet aching from the unaccustomed tightness of boots, his bad knee throbbing, Beecher limped up the steps of headquarters. The sign on the door read:

COL. HENRY C. BANKHEAD
POST COMMANDER

Beecher walked into an outer office which smelled of fresh cedar planking. The sergeant major arose and pointed to a closed door. "In there, sir. They're expecting you."

With a last-minute tug at his blouse, Beecher squared his shoulders and turned the knob. As the door swung inward he saw five men seated at a table—Colonel Bankhead, Major George Forsyth, two scouts in rough frontier garb—Sharp Grover and Bill Comstock—and General Sheridan. Beecher had never met Sheridan, but there was no mistaking Little Phil's identity. He was short and stout, harsh-featured, with a bushy mustache curving down over his mouth, his nose like an eagle's beak.

For some unaccountable reason, Beecher recalled President Lincoln's description of Sheridan: *A brown chunky little chap, with a long body, short legs, not enough neck to hang him, and such long arms that if his ankles itch he can scratch them without stooping.*

They were all staring at Beecher, and he felt his throat tightening against his words: "Lieutenant Beecher reporting, sir."

"Come in, come in." Sheridan's voice was gruff but kind. He offered his hand. "I'm General Sheridan. You know my aide, Major Forsyth?"

"We met last month, sir."

"And of course you know Colonel Bankhead and scouts Grover and Comstock."

"Very well indeed, sir."

They sat down, Beecher taking the empty chair at the end of the table, facing the general.

"Young man," Sheridan continued, "I once heard your uncle orate."

"Uncle Henry?"

"Henry Ward Beecher. A real spellbinder." Sheridan chuckled hoarsely, and placed his fleshy hands on the table before him. "You've done a fine job here at Fort Wallace with building construction, Lieutenant." His large penetrating eyes fixed on Beecher, who murmured politely: "Thank you, sir."

"Now the Army wants to try you at something different."

"Yes, sir?"

"Let me review our situation. General Grant sent me out here this spring with orders to see that the Medicine Lodge treaty of last autumn is enforced to the letter. That means of course that all this country between the Arkansas and Platte rivers is to be cleared of Indians, opened for settlement and peaceable completion of the Kansas Pacific Railroad to Denver. Leaders of four tribes agreed to this in exchange for reservation lands in the Indian Territory. Right now most of our cavalry troops are engaged to the south in this movement of peaceable tribes. So far so good. But Grover and Comstock, here, tell me we can still expect plenty of trouble, especially from Roman Nose and his Cheyennes."

"Roman Nose blooded us pretty bad right here a year ago last June," Grover said. The scout was lean and swarthy from his years on the plains, and when he spoke his face was without expression.

Colonel Bankhead added: "We lost seven men in that fight, and took fourteen severe casualties."

"Yes." Sheridan's eyes squinted thoughtfully. "This summer we shan't wait for the hostiles to come to us. In the first place, let's hope they've learned their lesson and will stay out of our settlement strip. If they do come in, we'll first try persuasion, the velvet glove."

"That might work with some holdouts, General," Bill Comstock commented. "Like Chief Turkey Leg, maybe. But not runagates like Two Crows or old Roman Nose. They and their wild bucks aim to kill or be killed."

Grover nodded his head in solemn agreement. "Roman Nose won't ever lead his warriors in to a reservation, no, sir, General."

"Very well. Now, that brings us around to you, Lieutenant Beecher. If we're going to be forced to deal with hostiles, I want to know their movements, their whereabouts, their intentions, the strength of their war parties. To a dot. I want to be one jump ahead of them all the time, and be ready to subdue them if necessary with superior forces."

Beecher was still puzzled as to what role he was expected to play in the general's plan. His face must have betrayed his uncertainty, for Sheridan spoke up sharply: "I suppose you consider this a large order, Lieutenant."

"Frankly, sir, I do. These hostiles have a tendency to break off in small bands. It isn't easy to predict what they'll do."

Sheridan nodded. "I know that. But the frontier Army can certainly do better than it has been doing in finding out where large concentrations of hostiles are. In the Civil War we called it spying."

Beecher smiled slightly. "I understand, sir."

"That will be your new assignment, Lieutenant."

"I, sir? Is the general aware of my physical condition?"

Sheridan thumped the table with one hand. "Of course I know. I know all about you, Mr. Beecher. You're an excellent horseman. You know almost as much about the tribes out here as Grover and Comstock. You are well educated, you are intelligent, you use excellent judgment. I've looked into your record."

Beecher's face had turned beet-red. "I beg your pardon, sir, for my question."

Sheridan chuckled, then continued: "You'll have assistance, of course. Grover and Comstock have agreed to serve under you. You'll be authorized to employ more scouts to work in pairs out of Forts Larned and Dodge."

Comstock spoke up: "Dick Parr over at Fort Hays would be a good man, General, and Buffalo Bill Cody if you could get him."

"Frank Espey and Wild Bill Hickok," Grover added.

"Lieutenant Beecher will choose his men," Sheridan said gruffly. "Now gentlemen, if there are no questions, we'll call this meeting adjourned."

Chairs scraped on the plank flooring. As Beecher arose, he was keenly aware of the stiffness in his bad knee, and wondered if he should not speak out and say honestly that he did not think he was the right man for the assignment.

He was turning toward the door when Sheridan's rough voice filled the room: "Lieutenant, just a moment. Before I instruct my adjutant to write your orders, I'd like a word with you in private."

"Yes, sir."

The others were gone, the door closing behind Major Forsyth. Sheridan asked coldly: "Do you have any doubts, Mr. Beecher?"

Beecher hesitated for a second. "No, sir. I'll do my best."

"Actually most of your work will be moving around the triangle of Forts Wallace, Larned, and Dodge. Keep your eyes and ears open. See that your scouts come in to these posts on regular schedules, and make certain they comb all the country between the Solomon and Arkansas rivers. I'll be at Fort Hays most of the time, and will expect a report from you at least once a week."

"Yes, sir."

"I shan't think of your scouts as spies, Lieutenant, but as mediators. Urge them to attempt persuasion as well as to gather information. I assume you have confidence in Grover and Comstock?"

"The utmost, sir. They've taught me a great deal."

"So I understand. Do you have any final questions?"

Beecher smiled. "Only one, General Sheridan. Of all the ambitious young lieutenants out here, why did you select a lame one?"

Sheridan shook his head. "I should think you'd be proud of your wounds, Mr. Beecher. But if you must have the truth, I'll give it to you. It was not I who chose you."

Beecher opened his mouth, unable to find words as Sheridan broke into a bellow of laughter. "That pair of rawhide scouts said they wouldn't serve under any officer but Lieutenant Beecher."

"Well, I'll be—" Beecher blushed, and then could not help but join General Sheridan in laughter. "The ornery rascals," he said. "Bill Comstock and Sharp Grover."

2

ABNER
(sharp) GROVER

May–August 1868

His name was Abner, but nobody ever used it. He was Sharp—Sharp Grover—and the name suited him. His friends among the other scouts admitted he had the sharpest eyes and ears of any plainsman they had known.

Nobody knew much about Sharp Grover. He spoke only when he felt the need for speech, and frontiersmen never pried into a man's past. He had been a trapper in the northwest, had married into the Sioux tribe, then drifted south to Army posts on the plains where he was in constant demand as a scout. It was said that his mother had been part French, part Indian, but even Grover's closest friend, Bill Comstock, did not know whether this was true or not.

On a warm morning in May 1868, Grover, Comstock, and Lieutenant Beecher were in the Fort Wallace trading post, waiting for the stagecoach which was to take them east to the railhead at Sheridan City where they would board a train for Fort Hays. The two scouts were in buckskins, Beecher in uniform. They sat on a wooden bench right-angled to the open entranceway.

None was in the mood for talk, and a casual passerby might have thought them total strangers to each other. Only their eyes revealed their alertness. Nothing that passed upon the Fort Wallace parade escaped their attention.

The silence was broken by the sound of moccasins padding on the hard earth outside. Four Sioux warriors appeared in the trading store entrance, hesitating a moment before entering. Grover's eyes scanned them with unhurried casualness, his ears understanding every harsh syllable of their Dakota tongue. They had come to barter buffalo robes and moccasins for sugar.

The post trader cleared a space on his counter, and the warriors laid out their goods for inspection.

"Twelve pints of sugar," the post trader said, pointing to a robe.

Grover's voice cut across the long room: "That one's worth fifteen and you know it."

The trader frowned back at the scout. "All right. Fifteen pints." He held up ten fingers, then five. The Sioux nodded agreement.

Lieutenant Beecher winked at Grover. He reached down and patted his tight boots. "Pick me out a pair of moccasins, Sharp," he said. "I intend to ease my feet out of these leathers as soon as we're off the post."

The three men arose and walked to the counter, where Grover selected a pair of soft black-beaded deerskins sewed expertly to thick rawhide soles. "Try these," he said to Beecher.

Beecher sat on the floor, grunting as he pulled off his army boots. In a matter of seconds, the scouts and the Indians joined him, sitting crosslegged, forming a circle. One of the older Sioux produced a pipe, filled it with tobacco, and there was no bargaining until the smoking pipe passed around the circle. The old Indian said something in Sioux.

"This one asks why soldier chief wants moccasins," Grover said.

"Tell him my feet ache," Beecher replied. He raised his trouser leg and exposed his scarred knee, then lowered his sock. His foot had healed badly.

The Indians grunted with admiration. Beecher patted his hip.

"Here, too," he said in English, but making the sign Grover had taught him, moving his extended index finger briskly toward his body and turning it so the tip just grazed the surface of his hip, like a glancing bullet.

The Indians murmured again, and the old one spoke slowly in Sioux.

"He will trade for tobacco," Grover said.

"How much tobacco?" Beecher asked.

The Sioux spoke again.

"For a brave soldier chief with many wounds," Grover translated, and grinned at Beecher. "It is for you to decide, Lieutenant."

"Five pounds?"

"A plenty." Grover turned his face toward the open doorway, his eyes squinting across the sunlit flats where a swirl of dust marked the trail to Cheyenne Wells. "Stagecoach coming," he announced.

On the jolting stage to Sheridan City the three men sat elbow to elbow, nodding, yawning and napping, but exchanging scarcely a word. Waiting for them at the railhead was a shiny black locomotive attached to two dull-red wooden coaches. The passengers alighted, pausing briefly while the driver tossed down their blanket rolls and saddlebags, and then strode toward the train.

Smoke boiled from the bulging stack of the locomotive. "Look at that panting varmint," Bill Comstock said, and held his nose. "Smells like the Stinking Springs up in Dakota country. This'll be my first train ride, Sharp. How about you?"

"I rode one a piece out of St. Louis once," Grover replied. He was thinking about the Indians, how they hated the iron horses which ran with such a clatter across the plains, frightening away buffalo herds and bringing settlers from the East. But that was life, always changing. If a man, white or Indian, couldn't change with it, he was doomed. The plains Indians had two choices—go north to the Powder River country, or south to reservations in Indian Territory. No use fighting it by turning runagate. Roman Nose and Turkey Leg, and Charley Bent and the Dog Soldier Cheyennes—

they wouldn't give up. They could still make plenty of trouble if they put their crazy minds to it.

The rocketing passenger train hustled them over a hundred miles of track to Fort Hays in five hours, which was better than stagecoach time ever was, and before midnight they were bedded down in a barracks. As Grover drifted off to sleep, he had to stop to remember where he was, and he wondered if mankind had not speeded things up a little too much.

Next day, he and Bill Comstock selected a pair of horses from the Fort Hays corral and jogged off north to scout the Saline River valley. Through June and July they worked the country around Forts Hays and Harker, reporting in regularly to Lieutenant Beecher. They found a few small bands of Cheyennes and Arapahos moving south to Indian Territory, but no traces of hostile marauders. All rumors they could pick up from the friendlies indicated that Roman Nose and the Dog Soldiers were still somewhere far to the north, hunting buffalo along the Platte.

Late in July they met Beecher at Fort Zarah. "My reports to General Sheridan are getting skimpier every week," the lieutenant complained. "You scouts know anything I can pass on to him?"

"It's been a quiet summer," Bill Comstock observed.

"We heard Turkey Leg's bunch is camped up Walnut Creek," Grover said.

"Rather far south for him," Beecher replied. "Perhaps he's changed his mind and aims to go on to the reservation."

"Not the way we heard it," Grover said.

Beecher shrugged. "Maybe the three of us can talk him into it. I'll ride out with you in the morning."

After three days of trailing west, they found a camp site only recently abandoned. Grover poked around in the dead ashes, peering and sniffing, circling the yellowed grass spots where tepees had stood. "Turkey Leg's band all right," he declared. "They went north."

"Too bad," Beecher said. "We'll follow them."

Next morning a cavalry patrol out of Fort Hays cut across their path. The horse soldiers were dead beat from too many hours in the saddle, their captain grumpy and gruff of voice. "Two days out and no sign of a redskin," he told Beecher. "The ground must've swallowed 'em up."

"What redskins you looking for?" Grover asked.

"Haven't you heard?" the captain demanded sourly.

"We've been down on Walnut Creek," Beecher explained.

"Marauding Cheyennes hit a bunch of ranchers and settlements along the Saline. Wiped out several families. Their sign pointed south."

Beecher glanced at Comstock. "Your quiet summer's over, Bill. Captain, the only Indian sign we've seen for miles is this trail we're following north. Turkey Leg's band."

"Maybe Turkey Leg did it," the captain said.

"Couldn't have," Grover replied. "His bunch is just about now coming in to the Saline country."

Beecher nodded. "Sharp's right. Of course this trouble means we have to find Turkey Leg in a hurry. Keep his young bucks away from the hostiles, talk him into turning south if we can. You heading back for Hays, Captain?"

The cavalry officer stood in his stirrups and stretched himself. "Might as well. If you scouts saw nothing south of here."

"We'll ride along with you."

They rode into Fort Hays on August 14, finding it full of rumors and empty of soldiers. All infantry and cavalry units were in the field. A report had just come in from Captain Fred Benteen's 7th Cavalry detachment. Benteen had overtaken a large force of hostiles, driving them for ten miles up the Saline.

"It'll be risky for three white men to go into that country now," Beecher said. Learning that General Sheridan was at Fort Wallace, he decided to telegraph him for further orders.

Within an hour Sheridan's reply came back over the wire. Beecher was to report to Fort Wallace immediately in person. Grover and Comstock were to scout up the Saline valley, using their discretion in parleying with Indians.

Grover listened to the reading of the telegram, remaining silent for a minute or so. "Bill and me, we'll be safe enough once we step inside Turkey Leg's tepee. May take some tricky work sneaking in there though. You game for it, Bill?"

Comstock nodded. "I trust old Turkey Leg, same as you, Sharp. If you're for it, I am."

"Good luck," Beecher told them, and they shook hands. "See you at Fort Wallace."

West of Fort Hays, the scouts picked up Turkey Leg's trail again, following it north to Solomon River. This was open country, buffalo country, still empty of settlements. On the morning of the second day, August 16, near the willow-fringed stream they found an abandoned camp no more than a day old. Grover pulled his horse over to one side, studying the tracks, then dismounted.

"Bill," he said. "Look here."

Comstock dropped from his saddle. "Pony tracks. Unshod. They come from across the river."

"A hundred maybe. Wild bucks from up north."

Comstock grunted. "If they joined on, too bad."

The scouts mounted and circled the hoof-marked ground. Only one trail led out across the prairie. The buffalo grass was still trodden down and bent in the direction of movement upriver. For a quarter of a mile ahead the sign was plain as day, the stretch of disturbed grass a different shade of green from that around it. "They joined on," he said. "Won't be healthy for us, going into Turkey Leg's next camp."

Comstock pulled a piece of dried beef from a pocket of his buckskins and chewed reflectively. "My medicine's been bad since yesterday, Sharp."

Grover's teeth showed in a flicker of a smile. "Old Medicine Bill. You're worse'n any medicine man, worrying about signs. What's wrong now?"

"My compass," Comstock replied. He turned the metal case tied by rawhide cord to a buttonhole in his shirt. "Needle's been spinning like crazy."

"Don't mean a thing." Grover squinted at the sun. "You want to bear off for Fort Wallace?"

Comstock shook his head. "We come this far, might as well pay a visit to Turkey Leg."

Late in the day they sighted the Indian camp. Grover pulled his rifle out of its boot and slipped it into a piece of leather slung over his saddle pommel, balancing the weapon horizontally across his legs. If he needed it in a hurry, all he had to do was raise it, aim, and fire.

They rode in a steady trot toward the curved line of tepees, slowing to a walk when they reached the fringes of the camp. A pack of dogs swirled out of nowhere, yipping at their horses' heels. They moved on around the first ellipse of tepees, where young warriors gathered quickly to stare with open hostility at these unannounced visitors.

"Not a friendly face in the bunch," Grover said softly. Riding knee to knee the scouts headed straight for the tepee in the center. It was marked with thunderbirds in bright yellows and reds.

"They'd cut our hearts out if they took a notion," Comstock replied.

Turkey Leg heard their horses' hoofbeats and flung back the flap of his tepee as the scouts were dismounting. His bronzed face, wrinkled by sun, wind and time, was solemn as he offered a formal greeting.

"I do not see a smile of welcome upon the face of my old friend," Grover said in Cheyenne.

"In these days a Cheyenne chief has no reason for smiling," Turkey Leg replied. With a graceful motion of his arm he indicated that they should enter the tepee. "Only in the lodge of Turkey Leg is a white man safe in this camp." As Grover bent to enter, he glanced back. Young warriors were gathering in small groups, watching them. Some lifted their blankets over their faces or turned their backs in gestures of animosity.

A fire was burning in the center of the tepee, a blue spiral lifting to the blackened smokehole. They sat around the small blaze while Turkey Leg prepared a pipe. "Why have you come here?" the chief asked.

"To speak for the Great Father's bluecoat soldiers," Grover answered. "It was written at Medicine Lodge that all the tribes would leave this country and go to the territory of the Indians."

Turkey Leg nodded gravely and touched a hand to his chest. "I did not sign it, but even so I would go. Many winters lie heavy upon Turkey Leg and he is for peace in a land where there are no white men. But my young warriors have spoken against this. They will stay and hunt in the land of their fathers."

"The bluecoat soldiers will not stand still for this." Grover took the offered pipe, turned it to the four directions, drawing puffs of smoke. "The soldiers are as many as grasshoppers in the Drying Grass Moon. They will come and drive your young men like cattle."

Turkey Leg drew in a puff of smoke, exhaling slowly. "If I turned toward the territory of the Indians at the next sun's rising, only a handful of old men and women would follow me. I am chief and must stay with my people."

Comstock pulled a sheaf of grass from the ground and tossed it on the fire where it flared and disappeared. "Your people will go like that, Turkey Leg. No medicine can stop it."

"We will wait and see," the chief answered.

"At your last camping place," Grover said, "many young warriors joined your people."

Turkey Leg looked directly at the scout, his eyes unblinking. "They are Cheyennes, as are my people."

"From Roman Nose?"

For the first time a faint smile showed on the old chief's lips. "My friend knows much. Yes, Roman Nose is coming south again as he did last summer. With many warriors and many new rifles. The Sioux and Arapaho are with him."

Grover shook his head. "He will lead your young men to die."

"They say Roman Nose has sworn to stop the iron horse from crossing the prairies. They say he will drive out all the settlers from the buffalo country."

Comstock made a scoffing sound in his throat. "Not even Roman Nose can do that."

Shadows from the firelight deepened the wrinkles in Turkey Leg's face. "Roman Nose has strong medicine," he declared. "He has been in many battles, but no white man's bullet has ever harmed him."

"All medicine turns bad," Comstock replied somberly, his fingers touching his dangling compass.

Grover tried once more: "Bring your people with us to Fort

Wallace. I can promise you rations and soldiers to protect you on the way to Indian Territory."

For a few moments the chief was silent, his face revealing no emotion. Then suddenly he brought his open right hand down sharply against the extended fingers of his left.

"That cuts it off," Comstock whispered. "He ain't going, nohow, Sharp."

Turkey Leg was already on his feet.

"It's near sundown," Grover said as he arose. "We'll camp here till morning."

The chief shook his head. "My old friends must go now, far out on the prairie. The young warriors from Roman Nose have sworn death to your people. My son will ride out with you. You will not be attacked in his presence."

Grover glanced at Comstock, who nodded quick agreement. "We'll ride," Grover said. Both scouts offered their hands in farewell, and Grover led the way outside.

The crowd of sullen-faced warriors had grown larger, thirty or more young men wearing blue or dark red blankets, some carrying rifles. At a sign from Turkey Leg, one of them came forward. His black hair was loose on his shoulders. A single feather and a beaded thong of rawhide hung from a plaited knot on top of his head. There was no formal introduction, only a quick exchange of Cheyenne monosyllables, and Grover understood that this young man was the chief's son. He and four others would stake their honor to escort the two scouts safely from the village.

Grover knew that under different circumstances these same five braves would have been equally honor-bound to kill him and Bill Comstock, but he also knew there would be little danger now until the chief's son had carried out the duty assigned him by his father.

As their horses trotted southward, the sun lay on their right, huge and orange in color, a few minutes above the flat horizon. They rode until dusk, the chief's son taking the lead, two warriors on either side of Grover and Comstock. In all this time not one word was said, the Indians ignoring the presence of their unwanted guests. With every passing minute, Grover became more alert, listening, looking. He knew that half a dozen other warriors were in the rear, keeping their ponies to the same pace as the escort.

Suddenly the chief's son halted, danced his pony around, slashed his hand down in a gesture of farewell, and the escort turned back for the village. The little group of warriors in the rear slowed for a minute or so until the returning escort passed them. Glancing back, Grover saw these other riders quirting their ponies; they were coming on now at a gallop.

Comstock said: "Reckon we ought to run for it, Sharp?"

"No use," Grover answered. "Let's see what they want."

They were seven, most of them so young they could scarcely be considered as warriors. The oldest one carried a carbine slung over his back, a new Sharps breechloader. On his leggings he wore tiny bells which jingled with a silvery sound. Overtaking the scouts, they trotted alongside, shouting mild insults in Cheyenne.

For a minute or so the scouts ignored the taunts, continuing in their steady trot while twilight deepened around them. Then Grover began answering the Indians, returning jibe for jibe, teasing them but avoiding direct insults. One of the younger braves laughed, the others joining in.

Grover breathed easier. In ten more minutes the rolling land would be closed in darkness and a showdown surely would be avoided. He signaled Comstock to increase speed; they nudged their horses into a gallop.

In a few seconds the slower Indian ponies fell back. The seven Cheyennes were strung out now, only the rider with the belled leggings keeping pace, and then he swerved his pony and turned away, shouting a final jeering remark.

Grover kept one hand on his balanced rifle, listening to the fading hoofbeats, alert for any unusual sound. The sound came like an unexpected handclap, repeated, and as he identified it he felt the searing fire of a bullet tearing into his left shoulder.

He whirled in his saddle, his rifle up, firing at running shadows against the purple sky. Bill Comstock's horse slammed against his leg. The saddle was empty.

"Bill!" Grover dismounted quickly, forgetting his wound until he winced from pain, and in that half second of motion he lost rein and bridle. His horse darted away after Comstock's.

North on the darkening prairie he heard a faint silvery jingle of legging bells, and he caught a quick flash of orange fire. He hit the ground as a bullet screamed past, followed by the cracking echo of a rifle.

For several seconds he lay flat, then raised his head above the thick grass, his eyes straining in the dim light. A few yards up the trail he saw a dark shadow, and began crawling toward it. Before he was halfway there, he knew it was Comstock.

At the sound of hoofbeats far off to his right, he stopped. The Cheyennes were after his and Comstock's horses. "Bill!" he called softly. "They've gone. You all right?"

There was no answer. Grover raised himself to his knees, running forward in a stooping position. As soon as he touched Comstock's face he knew he was dead, and he felt a surge of bitter anger. The Cheyennes had no better friend among the white men than Bill Comstock, and now they had killed him.

For a minute or more Grover kneeled there, and then out of the darkness he heard the ponies coming back at a full gallop. Instinctively he rolled away, seeking cover against a hummock of buffalo grass. He lay on his side, gripping his rifle, watching blurred shadows moving against the night sky. The riders made a wide circle, slowed their pace, and he counted seven riders, nine horses. They'd captured the scouts' mounts.

Tiny bells tinkled, and he turned his rifle toward the sound, his fingers curving on the trigger. A few Cheyenne words floated out of the darkness. He heard the slap of rawhide against horseflesh, and they were galloping again, back toward Turkey Leg's camp.

Maybe they'd come back, maybe not. There was nothing for it now but to walk, and walk fast. He reached under his buckskin and found the shoulder of his woolen shirt saturated with blood which was still oozing from the bullet hole. To stop the flow, he ripped a strip from his shirt and balled it into the wound.

By now the sky was filled with stars. He found the Big Dipper, turned his back on the North Star, and started walking south. If the Cheyennes did not come back, and if he could keep going long enough, sooner or later he would reach the railroad.

At the first light of dawn, Grover sighted a line of eroded clay formations off to the west, and knew that he was near Monument Station. He would have turned in that direction, knowing a telegrapher was there, but his strength was too far gone. The railroad was closer, only two or three more miles straight south, and he kept the same course he had followed all night, resting every few hundred steps, struggling onward until at last he saw the shining tracks of the railroad.

Crawling up the embankment, he pressed one ear against a rail, listening, but there was no sound. He drained the last drops of water from his canteen, then stretched out beside the railroad ties, pillowing his head on his good arm.

Before noon he was awakened by the chugging of a locomotive, the clacking of metal wheels against rail joints. With an effort he got upon his feet and began waving his hat. A moment later he saw steam jutting from each side of the rocking locomotive, heard the squeal of braked wheels sliding over rails.

The train was an empty work shuttle headed east for supplies. Its crewmen wasted no time helping Grover aboard. They made a canvas pallet for him in a freight car, and waited patiently for him to gather enough strength to tell his story. They also had news for him. Hostile Indians had struck an advance work camp of the railroad, wounding several of the construction crew, and there were rumors of other raids across the Colorado line.

Late that afternoon the train rolled to a stop beside the water tank near Fort Hays, and Grover dropped down on the graveled platform. His swollen shoulder throbbed and he felt hot with fever, but he had regained some of his strength. With a wave of thanks to the train crew, he started in a fast walk for the station down the track.

In front of the telegraph office, a lieutenant sat propped in a chair. He glanced twice at Grover before recognizing him. "Sharp!" he called, and rocked forward to his feet. "What happened to you?"

"I'll tell you as soon as you clear a telegraph line to Fort Wallace."

"You ought to see a surgeon first." The lieutenant stared at the dried blood on Grover's buckskins and undershirt.

"You send a message to Lieutenant Beecher, then I'll see a sawbones."

The lieutenant held the door open. Inside, a signal corporal was jotting down a message coming in dots and dashes over a chattering sounder in front of him. Grover and the lieutenant stood patiently for a minute or so until the sound stopped.

"Another Indian raid on Pond Creek," the corporal said. "Killed a woman and two children. General Sheridan is ordering all spare troops to move out of Hays."

The lieutenant took the message sheet, read it, and shook his head. "Nothing left in here now but a garrison guard. Corporal, clear your line to Fort Wallace. Sharp Grover here has an urgent message for Lieutenant Beecher."

Grover sat down in a cane-bottomed chair offered him by the lieutenant and began telling the corporal what he wanted in the message. When he finished, the lieutenant was gone but he reappeared in a few moments. "I told my messenger to round up a surgeon for you."

Grover leaned back in the chair, letting his tired muscles relax. His shoulder felt as if it had a red hot poker in it.

Half an hour passed before the messenger returned with a doctor.

"What took you so long?" the lieutenant growled.

"All post surgeons are in the field, sir," the messenger replied. "I found a civilian doc in Hays City."

The doctor pushed his way inside and dropped his leather bag on the floor in front of Grover's chair. He had heavy black eyebrows and a short chin beard. "I'm John Mooers. You must be the wounded scout."

Grover leaned forward to let Mooers assist in removing his buckskin and undershirt. With gentle fingers the doctor examined the wound. "Bullet went clean through. You're lucky. A little carbolic acid, Mr. Grover. It'll burn a bit."

After strapping bandages around the shoulder, Mooers smiled. "A week in bed, and you'll be good as new."

The corporal swung around on his swivel chair. "Reply to your message, Mr. Grover."

"What does it say?"

" 'Grieved to hear of Bill Comstock's death. General Sheridan has ordered cavalry to Solomon Valley to pursue Turkey Leg's band. Will try to recover Comstock's body. General Sheridan orders you to report to Fort Wallace immediately. Fred Beecher, Lieutenant.' "

Grover nodded. "When's the next train west?"

"Six o'clock in the morning," the lieutenant answered. "Didn't you inform Beecher you were badly wounded?"

"No." Grover's teeth showed in a flash of a smile. "I can rest up on that train."

Dr. Mooers shook his head. "You ought to be in hospital, Mr. Grover. That bullet may have got a piece of your lung."

"Bill Comstock's dead," Grover replied bitterly. "I figure I owe him all I can do, and that's to help the Army punish his killers. The Army needs me at Fort Wallace."

Late the next day, Grover was on the regular stage when it stopped in front of the post trading store at Fort Wallace. Lieutenant Beecher was waiting for him.

Beecher frowned when he saw the scout's arm in a sling. "You didn't tell me about that," he said accusingly.

"Nothing but a scratch," Grover replied.

"You sure? You look pale around the eyes, Sharp."

"Too much sleep, I reckon."

"All right. Something big is in the wind for the scouts. I have orders to report with you to Major Sandy Forsyth."

3

MAJOR GEORGE
(SANDY) FORSYTH

August 24–25, 1868

Major George (Sandy) Forsyth was a handsome square-jawed man
in his early thirties, a veteran of four years of Civil War and three
years of uneasy peace in the South and West. Except for a mustache his face was clean-shaven, and he wore his straw-colored hair
much shorter than most frontier officers. His large expressive eyes
betrayed his impatience as he glanced frequently at a ticking clock
on the wall of Colonel Bankhead's office.

Bankhead, who was studying a map spread over his desk top,
looked up at him. "I believe I hear the stagecoach coming in now,
Sandy," he said.

Forsyth strode to a window and stared across the parade
ground. "Sure enough, there it is, half an hour late as usual." He
frowned. "Sharp was on it all right, but his arm's in a sling."

Bankhead joined him at the window. "Don't worry about that.
It would take more than a winged arm to stop Grover."

In less than five minutes there was a knock on the door and in
response to Bankhead's gruff "come in," Lieutenant Beecher and

Grover entered. The colonel kept his seat, but reached for a tin pitcher and poured two glasses of water. "You could probably do with stronger stuff, Sharp, but at least this is chilled from our ice-house." Grover picked up a glass and drank thirstily.

"Why didn't you inform us you'd been wounded?" the major asked, and then without waiting for a reply waved the scout and the lieutenant to a battered bench against the wall. "General Sheridan asked me to express his regrets to you personally, concerning your friend Bill Comstock."

Grover shook his head. "Bill didn't have a chance. Hostile Cheyennes had us ringed in. It was near dark, but I'm pretty sure Two Crows was leading the bunch."

"Two Crows?" Bankhead's face showed surprise. "He was with Roman Nose's outlaw band last year, wasn't he?"

"That's right, Colonel."

"Then Roman Nose must be somewhere around."

"I figger so." Grover shifted slightly on the bench to ease his wounded shoulder.

"Does that arm pain you?" Forsyth asked.

"I've had worse, Major."

Forsyth smiled faintly. "I suppose there's no need my going into the reasons why I want to see you and Fred Beecher. You both know that Indian attacks are increasing every day. We're so short of troops out here we can't protect the railroad work crews or the settlers. We'll have to try something new, and try it fast."

"Are no more troops to be assigned this department, sir?" Beecher asked quickly.

"Not even a company," Forsyth replied. "General Sheridan and I have discussed every possibility. We finally decided on this as a starter." He drew a folded sheet of yellow paper from his blouse pocket and held it out to Beecher. "The general issued the order much quicker than I expected him to, but that's his way. I'd like to know frankly what you and Sharp Grover think of the practicalities."

Beecher unfolded the yellow flimsy and read the order aloud:

Major George H. Forsyth: The general commanding directs that you, without delay, employ fifty first-class hardy frontiersmen, to be used as scouts against the hostile Indians, to be commanded by yourself, with Lieutenant Beecher, 3rd Infantry, your subordinate. You can enter into such articles of agreement with these men as will compel obedience.

As he finished, Beecher gave Forsyth a look of admiration. "A splendid idea, sir. I shall be honored to serve in your command." He smiled. "This certainly proves there's more than one way to raise a company of soldiers."

"Not soldiers, Lieutenant. Scouts. We're not authorized to recruit soldiers, so let's not forget to keep this within regulations." Forsyth's eyes twinkled. "What do you think, Mr. Grover? We're counting on you to ride as chief of scouts."

Grover replied slowly, as though choosing his words carefully: "I reckon you can round up fifty good scouts, Major, but they won't likely take to having commands shouted at them. Some of the best of these fellows have done their army time in the war, and they don't want no more of a uniform. You find a good scout, you also find a pretty independent codger. Got his own notions about doing things. Plain ornery sometimes."

"How about you?"

"Oh, count me in on it, if Fred Beecher's the lieutenant."

"Good. Now I think we'd better clear up a few points. In the first place, Mr. Grover, the scouts will wear what they please. No uniforms. Our primary purpose will be to locate the main camps of these small bands of hostiles who are doing all the raiding. If challenged by war parties, we shall fight them, but our main objective is to locate their big camps. Once they are located, I shall dispatch scouts to the nearest forts to bring up enough soldiers to defeat or force these hostiles to surrender. As it is now we have companies marching all over the plains searching for Indians but traveling so slowly and stirring up so much dust and noise that the Indians constantly elude them. When our soldiers do pick up a fresh trail and start in pursuit, the marauders separate, turn off by twos and threes from the main party and scatter. They're tricky and dangerous, and have more and better horses than our cavalry. Our green troopers can beat them any time in a standup fight, but they don't know enough about prairie craft to go after the hostiles in twos and threes. For the same reason they're not much good at courier work, either. We need men who know the country, who know how the Indian fights as an individual. You see what I'm driving at?"

Beecher was leaning forward, listening intently. "Yes, sir," he answered. Grover squinted at the ceiling a moment, and drawled: "Suppose we do find a hostile village, Major? Them Indians are not going to just sit in their lodges while our messengers go riding for soldiers. Wild bucks get mighty touchy when their squaws are in danger. They'll either come out and fight us or break camp and skedaddle fast."

"If they attack us," Forsyth replied, "we'll defend ourselves until help comes. If they run, we'll keep on their tails and keep the soldiers informed where they are."

Still nodding his head, the scout eased his wounded shoulder against the back of the bench. "Might be worth a try at that."

Colonel Bankhead spoke for the first time: "It strikes me as about the only way we can stop them, Sharp. And we have to do it quickly. Every settler and rancher, every workman in the railroad construction camps has heard of Roman Nose's boast that he and his Dog Soldiers will stop the iron horse or die in the attempt. Two or three more dirty raids, and the railroad builders will pack up and go, and not another foot of rail will be laid."

Grover's only indication that he had been listening was a loud sigh. "Course you can't blame them buffalo-hunting Dog Soldiers—"

The major's voice cut in harshly: "If you don't think our plan will work—" A knock on the door interrupted his retort.

"Come in!" Colonel Bankhead shouted.

A tall man with a bushy beard stood in the open doorway. "Am I interrupting something?" he asked apologetically.

"No, no." Forsyth arose quickly. "Come in, McCall."

"Your messenger just now found me," the tall man explained. "We were out in the hayfield."

Forsyth introduced the new arrival to the others. "William Mc-

Call outranks all of us," he said. "He was breveted a brigadier general during the last Virginia campaign."

McCall shrugged. "Out here, Civil War rank doesn't carry much weight unless you're in uniform."

Lieutenant Beecher made room for him on the bench, and asked: "Weren't you back at Fort Harker early in the summer?"

"Yes, I was clerking in the sutler's store. We unemployed generals take our work where we can find it."

Forsyth drew a pipe from his pocket and began tamping tobacco into the bowl. "I hope you've decided to come in with us, McCall."

The veteran of Virginia campaigning rubbed his fingers over his unkempt beard. "I suppose I'll have to give this brush a military cut, Major. As I see it, better a first sergeant than a forgotten general."

"Excellent!" Forsyth lighted his pipe, puffing out a cloud of smoke.

Colonel Bankhead applauded by slapping his desk top with the palm of his hand. "Gentlemen, may I offer my congratulations and best wishes to the staff of Sandy Forsyth's Scouts. Major Forsyth, Lieutenant Beecher, First Sergeant McCall, and Chief of Scouts Grover."

"Thank you, sir," replied Forsyth, "and thank you, gentlemen. General Sheridan will be delighted when he learns how quickly you've all responded." He pointed his pipe stem at Grover. "Even though our chief of scouts seems to have some reservations."

"I told you, Major, I thought it was worth a try." Grover's tone was peevish. "Could I have another drink of that cold water?"

Forsyth reached for the tin pitcher, and when he handed the glass to Grover he peered closely at the scout's face and then gently touched a hand against his forehead. "You're burning up with fever, Mr. Grover. Come along, we're going to the hospital."

Next afternoon after a dreary ride on one of the railroad's work trains, Major Forsyth, Lieutenant Beecher, and First Sergeant Mc-Call established a recruiting office in the quartermaster warehouse at Fort Harker. Sharp Grover, although protesting vigorously, had finally agreed to remain for a week in the Fort Wallace hospital. It was he who suggested Fort Harker as a recruiting station because of the large number of buffalo hunters, teamsters, bullwhackers, and scouts who used it as a base.

Forsyth had telegraphed ahead to the post commander, announcing the plan to organize a company of scouts. Before former Brigadier General McCall could trim his beard, get fitted for a new sergeant's uniform, and obtain a muster-book with pen and ink, more than a dozen hard-bitten plainsmen were gathered outside the warehouse, eager to volunteer. They were of all ages, from unbearded youths to grizzled veterans, and they were dressed in everything from jeans to buckskins and leather breeches.

Inviting them all inside, the major patiently explained the purposes of the scouting company. "We have no authority to enlist you into the Army," he continued, "but General Sheridan has obtained funds to employ fifty scouts at seventy-five dollars per month if you furnish your own horse, fifty dollars per month if the Army furnishes the horse. If your horse is worn out or killed in service you will be paid full value for it. Only Lieutenant Beecher, Sergeant McCall, and I will wear uniforms. Scouts will dress as they please. The Army will furnish rations and equipment for men, forage for mounts. Each scout will be issued a Spencer seven-shot repeating carbine and a Colt Army revolver. Any questions?"

One man wanted to know how long they would be in service. "No definite term," Forsyth replied. "But we'll expect every man to stay with us and obey orders of the officers as long as we're scouting in the field." There were no more questions, and none of the prospective recruits made any move to leave. "All right, men, line up in front of Sergeant McCall's table. Lieutenant Beecher probably knows all of you or has heard of you. He'll choose the men he wants."

Beecher, who had been sitting on a wooden ammunition box, arose and limped along the line. He reached out to touch one man on the shoulder. "Dave, you couldn't last two days with this outfit and you know it." The man grinned sheepishly. "If you say so, Lieutenant. No harm trying." He dropped out and started for the door. Beecher stopped suddenly beside another applicant, leaning close to him. "Anderson, if you come in here sober tomorrow, we might give you a second chance." The man protested, but Beecher turned his back on him. "All right, Sergeant McCall, muster in the rest of them."

A young boy dressed in a fringed jacket, a pair of faded Kentucky jeans, and well-worn army boots appeared suddenly in the doorway near where Major Forsyth was standing. He had bright blue eyes and long auburn hair which fell over his forehead in curls. Removing his dusty wide-brimmed hat, he asked politely: "Is this where they're enlisting men for Major Forsyth's Scouts?"

Forsyth nodded, barely suppressing a smile. "Who do you want to see, son? I'm Major Forsyth."

The boy blinked his eyes. "I'd like to join on, sir."

"How old are you?"

"Nineteen."

"Fifteen or sixteen would be closer to the truth, wouldn't it?"

Shaking his head, the boy insisted he was nineteen. Lieutenant Beecher turned to look at him, and asked: "What's your name?"

"Simpson Stilwell, but most folks call me Jack."

"Have you ever scouted for the Army?"

"Last summer. Out of Fort Dodge."

"You've also hunted buffalo with Pete Trudeau?"

"Yes, sir."

Beecher glanced at Forsyth. "I've seen the lad around, Major. He might do."

"With those curls he looks like a girl," Forsyth replied sharply. "Can he ride and shoot?"

Young Stilwell held himself proudly erect. "As well or better than any of those fellows over there."

Forsyth frowned at Beecher. "If that boy is nineteen I'm old enough to be retired from service." He hesitated a moment. "All right Mr. Jack Stilwell, you bring your horse around here in the morning at seven o'clock on the dot. We'll have a look at what you can do."

The boy grinned and pushed his hat down over his mass of curly hair. "Thanks, Major, I'll be here as sure as my name's Jack Stilwell."

4

Jack Stilwell

As soon as he left the quartermaster warehouse, Jack Stilwell hurried past an empty barracks and turned down a dusty street which ended against a two-story wooden building. Crude black letters had been painted on the warped and weathered boards: *BASS STABLES*.

Seated in a rocking chair out front was a powerfully built man with reddish hair and beard. He was mending a section of harness. "Well, Jack," he asked, "did you join up?"

"Not yet, Mr. Bass. I'll need a horse first. If you'll let me have that claybank mustang, the Army will pay me twenty-five dollars extra a month."

"How much can *you* pay *me*?"

"I'll give you the twenty-five dollars a month."

The stableman laughed. "That mustang is my best horse, Jack. The fastest, surest-footed, long-windedest piece of horseflesh in Kansas."

"That's why I want him, Mr. Bass."

After completing a tie in a strip of rawhide, Bass peered over his steel-rimmed spectacles at the boy. "I'll think about it."

"But I'll need him in the morning."

Bass grumbled to himself for a minute or so. "You won't leave off pestering me till you get that claybank, will you? All right, you sign a paper to pay me twenty-five dollars a month for three months, he's yours."

"You're a square-shooter, Mr. Bass."

"Soft in the head is more like it."

"Will you do something else for me?"

Bass growled a fierce "No!" but Jack had bent down and picked up a pair of shears lying at the side of the chair. "Please sir, cut off some of my hair."

"Thunderation, boy, I'm not a barber!" He resisted the offered shears for a moment, then took them, shaking his head in disgust. "Hunker down here so I can get at you." He began snipping away at the long hair. "You're going to look like a sheared sheep." He held one of the curls between his fingers. "Mighty pretty. Bet I could pass this one off as a keepsake from a lady friend."

Jack ran his fingers gingerly over his head. "Pete Trudeau won't like this. He believes short hair on a man scares away the buffalo. Is he up in the room?"

"Yeah, he's been up there since noontime. Trying to make up his mind to join Forsyth's Scouts."

"I'll go up and convince him." He glanced at the pile of hair clippings on the dusty ground. "Could I take the mustang out for a ride later on?"

Bass sighed. "We'll talk about it at supper time, boy."

Late that night after Jack Stilwell had stretched out on the bunk in the room he shared with Pete Trudeau above the stables, he thought about what he must do the next morning. On that clay-bank mustang, he knew he could outride any man Major Forsyth chose to put against him. The shooting, however, worried him a little. If the major set up those Army bull's-eye targets he might not do so well. All his life he had been shooting at moving objects, had never seen much use in shooting at still targets, and he knew some of the soldiers were mighty good at bull's-eye shooting.

As he drifted off to sleep, he tried to count back so he would know for certain how old he was. He counted the summers, the first one when he left that little settlement on the Missouri River to work his way to Santa Fe on a wagon train, then the summer he was with the Mexicans down there rounding up wild horses, and had to learn Spanish so they could understand what he was saying. Then the summer he came back, and the two buffalo hunts. What a time he had then with Pete Trudeau and the Cheyenne friendlies! Had to learn some of their words, too. He figured up to five summers, counting this one, but the trouble was he could not remember whether he was thirteen or fourteen when he left the settlement, or maybe he was only twelve.

Across the room, he heard Pete stirring in his sleep, muttering something in French, and then he remembered nothing more until first daylight wakened him. Pete's bunk was empty.

While he was pulling on his boots, he heard footsteps on the stairway, and a moment later from the doorway Pete Trudeau's bright eyes were glaring at him above a flickering candle. Trudeau's mustache, side whiskers and bushy eyebrows were white in contrast to his shoulder-length black hair. "You sleep all day, you'll never be one of that major's scouts," he said gruffly.

"Are you going to join up, Pete?"

Trudeau blew out the candle. "If Jack go, old Pierre go. Without hair, you no good for hunting buffalo no more for a while."

Jack fastened his gun belt and reached for his hat. "I don't think Major Forsyth likes long hair."

"Then perhaps I will not go. It is bad medicine to go with a naked head looking for Indians."

"Ah, you're wrong, Pete. No Indian would waste his time trying to scalp me now, but they'd chase you clear to Leavenworth to get that mane you're wearing. Come on, let's go."

Long before seven o'clock they rode up to the quartermaster warehouse, Trudeau on a dust-colored mount, Jack on the mustang he had obtained from the Bass stables. The old plainsman dismounted at the tie rail, but the boy put the mustang into a fast trot up the parade ground, circling the flagpole at the end, and then came back down at a fast gallop. Recognizing Major Forsyth on the warehouse platform, he reined up. "Good morning, sir."

The major nodded. "That's a fine horse you've got there, young man."

"Would you like to see me put him through his paces?"

"I've seen enough. Go on inside and sign Sergeant McCall's book."

"You mean that, sir? You don't want to see me shoot?" Jack dropped off the mustang and looped a tie over the rail.

"Save your ammunition for the hostiles, son. If you'd told us yesterday you could understand Cheyenne talk—"

"You didn't ask me."

"And we wouldn't have known it yet if Lieutenant Beecher had not inquired around." He slapped the boy on the seat of his dusty jeans, propelling him through the doorway.

Inside, Jack found the warehouse crowded with scouts, many of them men he knew and who called his name as he entered. He pushed through to Sergeant McCall's table where two recruits were waiting. The younger one turned, grabbing him by the hand. "Jack Stilwell, you old coyote. You going with us?"

"Wouldn't miss it, Hutch."

"You know my pa, don't you?"

"How're you, Mr. Farley?" The older man shook hands warmly, but his eyes had a bleak look in them. Jack had heard the story of the Farleys. Not long back Cheyennes had raided their ranch, killing Mrs. Farley and two children. Only Lewis Farley and his son survived, and both had sworn to avenge the killings.

Sergeant McCall interrupted. "Sign your name there, Mr. Farley." He glanced at Jack. "Are you still sure you want to scout with us, young man?"

"Yes, sir."

"All right, your full name?"

Jack gave the sergeant his name, address, color of eyes, hair and complexion, and then declared firmly that he was nineteen years old. "Sign here," McCall said then, "and I'll swear all three of you into service at the same time."

After he had scribbled his name, Jack stood back beside the Farleys, and at Sergeant McCall's direction raised his right hand. "Do you Lewis Farley, Hudson Farley, and Simpson Jack Stilwell solemnly swear to obey all orders given you by the officers of Forsyth's Scouts?"

Their voices mingled in a variety of affirmations.

"Say 'I do,'" the sergeant cried impatiently.

"I do," they replied in a chorus.

Lieutenant Beecher appeared suddenly out of the restless crowd. "How many do you have now, Sergeant?"

McCall glanced at his muster book. "Forty exactly, sir."

"Then we'll stop enlistments. We've got the best of the lot here. The major just received a telegram from Fort Hays that at least a dozen good men are waiting to join us over there."

Jack spoke up quickly: "Lieutenant Beecher, will you take just one more—one of the best scouts in Kansas?"

"Who is he?"

"Pete Trudeau."

"Trudeau?" Sergeant McCall interrupted. "I mustered him in five minutes ago."

"That one's a real runagate," Beecher said, but he winked at Jack. "Stilwell, I'm going to give you your first order. Come with me and the sergeant down to the supply room. If we're going to march out of Fort Harker before noon, we've got to start outfitting this mangy bunch of prairie dogs."

Major Forsyth was waiting for them in the supply room at the opposite end of the warehouse. Stacks of blankets, carbines, pistols, saddles, and other gear filled most of the floor. In a few minutes Sergeant McCall had organized a line, and while he checked off the items Jack handed them out to the scouts.

Each man received a pair of army blankets, a Spencer repeating carbine, a Colt's revolver, 140 rounds of rifle and 30 rounds of revolver ammunition, a lariat and picket pin, a canteen, haversack, butcher knife, tin plate, tin cup, and cold rations for a two-day march. To those few who would use army mounts, a saddle and bridle also were issued.

"Pack your supplies, ready your horses, and form up on the

parade," Major Forsyth repeated as each man left the line. When the last scout was outfitted, Sergeant McCall closed his book. "As soon as you've collected a set of equipments for yourself," he told Jack, "bring that pile of supplies over there out the back way." He disappeared through the rear door.

When Jack brought the first load of supplies out on the back platform, he found McCall, Beecher, and two scouts there with four pack mules. Working rapidly, they soon had the mules loaded with camp kettles, bags of salt and coffee, medicine kits, picks and shovels, and a reserve supply of ammunition. The lieutenant made a careful inspection, shifting the loads slightly on the mules' backs, checking the ties, and then pronounced them ready to march. "How about you, Stilwell? Where's your mount?"

"Other side of the building, sir."

"Pack up, saddle up, and join the others. We're aiming to make sixty miles to Hays by tomorrow sundown."

Less than an hour later Forsyth's Scouts rode out of Fort Harker. Along the dusty street to the unpainted board-framed entranceway, the horsemen moved at a slow pace. Here and there a garrison soldier stared curiously at them; two children stopped their play to wave; an officer's wife walking on a graveled pathway tipped her parasol in a farewell salute. No band played; no guidons rippled in the warm breeze. At a command from Major Forsyth, they turned into the trail and headed west alongside the track of the new railroad with the glittering August sun burning into their shoulders.

It was long after dark before they halted along a tiny creek where so many others had camped before them that not a cottonwood or willow was left standing, and the scouts searched for an hour before they could find enough twigs to heat water for coffee. Jack Stilwell was thankful that Sergeant McCall spared him guard detail. He ate his cold bacon and hard bread, washed the food down with warm coffee, and curled up in his army blanket, content to be out on the prairie again.

Next morning they were in their saddles at four o'clock, moving steadily in the cool dawn. All day, Forsyth held rest stops to a minimum, and as the sun was setting they rode into Hays City.

Some of the scouts trotted their horses up to the head of the column, requesting permission to drop out for an evening of jollity, but Major Forsyth denied all requests. "When we reach the fort, Sergeant McCall will issue such leaves and passes as he sees fit."

Jack noticed that the irregular column was attracting considerable attention as it passed through the little town. On the board sidewalk in front of a shabby hotel he saw a familiar face, a boy about his own age, small and dark, watching intently. Where had he known him—Junction City, Salina? What was his name? Just as the face vanished in the dusty twilight, he remembered him—Slinger the little Jew—Sigmund Schlesinger.

5

SIGMUND SCHLESINGER

Before sunup, Sigmund Schlesinger was at the Hays City railroad depot where he went through his daily ritual of sorting newspapers dropped from the baggage car of the early morning train. Using a notebook as guide, he carefully wrote the name of each subscriber on the top margin of the front page of the appropriate paper from St. Louis, Chicago, or New York, and then tucked them neatly into a saddlebag.

Most of his customers were officers at Fort Hays, and after a hurried round of the Hays City business establishments, he started on the long walk out to the army post. Young Schlesinger did not mind the walk in the cool of the day, with birds singing on the prairie and the fresh smell of earth before the sun burned away the dew. Frequently along the way he shifted the heavy saddlebag from one shoulder to the other, and by the time he delivered his last papers at General Sheridan's headquarters, he was more than ready for breakfast.

He had an arrangement with the contract cook who supplied

meals to civilian workers at the fort. In exchange for washing dishes and cleaning the stoves, he received a free breakfast.

On this particular morning he was surprised to find the mess tent filled to capacity, and then he remembered that Forsyth's Scouts had marched in the night before. As he reached for a tin plate, somebody called his nickname: "Slinger!" He turned and there was Jack Stilwell grinning at him. "Jack!" They shook hands, each one asking the other if he had joined the scouts. "Do you think they would take me?" Schlesinger asked hopefully.

"Sure they will. I'll put in a word for you," Jack promised. They filled their plates from pans on a table, and because all benches were filled inside the tent they went outside and sat on the edge of a watering trough to eat their breakfasts. They talked about the time they had chopped and hauled wood together on Big Creek for an army contractor, and then brought each other up to date on what they had been doing since. "Nothing much," Schlesinger said. "Clerking in a store at Hays City, waiting tables at the hotel, night-herding mules for the railroad workers, peddling newspapers—nothing much. I left New York three years ago to find adventure out here in the West. I might as well have stayed back east."

"You come with me," Jack said. "Lieutenant Beecher and Sergeant McCall are recruiting more men right now."

Jack's optimism was contagious, and Schlesinger agreed to come as soon as he told the cook he would be back to clean up. He took the empty plates and hurried into the tent, returning a moment later with his saddlebag slung over one shoulder. "I wish I had a buckskin shirt like yours, Jack. In these store clothes, I don't look like a scout."

"That's no matter. This old buckskin is beginning to unravel anyway." He indicated a broken seam at the collar.

Schlesinger smiled. "You let me have that when I come back to the tent, and I'll fix it for you. I worked as a tailor before I came West."

"You know how to do everything, Slinger. Soon as we talk to Lieutenant Beecher, he'll swear you right in."

Beecher and McCall had established a recruiting office in a partially completed barracks. It was windowless and unfurnished, but by propping a few boards across packing boxes, they had made it adequate for their purposes.

When Schlesinger arrived under the confident sponsorship of Jack Stilwell, he was surprised to see Dr. Mooers, one of his Hays City newspaper customers. The doctor nodded a greeting, but continued his conversation with Lieutenant Beecher: "When I heard what you and the major were doing I made up my mind to offer my services."

"I'm sure Major Forsyth will be delighted to have a surgeon," Beecher said. "Here he comes now. Major, this is Dr. John Mooers. He just walked in here and volunteered to be our surgeon."

"That's the best news I've heard today," Forsyth declared. "We were expecting to find a dozen good men here at Hays to fill out our company, but the rascals have all departed."

"They went out after those Indian raiders north of here," Mooers said.

"Yes, the cavalry company that went in pursuit was so under strength they asked for civilian volunteers." Forsyth gave the doctor a quizzical look. "What makes you want to give up the comforts of civilian life, Dr. Mooers, to join this company of hardbitten scouts?"

"I suppose I started thinking about it the night I patched up Sharp Grover's shoulder. Something about the man's determination made me realize that none of us is safe out here until this senseless raiding is stopped. When I heard about Forsyth's Scouts, I knew I had to volunteer."

"So you were Grover's doctor? You did a good job on him. Have you had any military experience, Dr. Mooers?"

"I was in a New York regiment during the Civil War."

"That's good enough for me. When can you join us?"

"I need a few days to transfer my patients to a colleague in Hays City. He'll be a busy man until I return."

"We'll be marching out of here tomorrow to scout the Solomon River valley," Forsyth said. "But we should be at Fort Wallace about a week from now. Sharp Grover will join us there. Can you?"

"I'll be there," Mooers replied.

Sigmund Schlesinger, who had been listening with interest to the conversation, suddenly realized that Jack was tugging at his arm. "Lieutenant Beecher," Jack was saying, "I'd like you to know my friend, Slinger."

Beecher turned, his eyes friendly. "Oh, Sig Schlesinger. Delivered the *Herald* to me when I was here last spring. How's business?"

"Not good, sir. Most of my subscribers are out in the field these days."

"Slinger wants to join us," Jack said quickly.

The lieutenant looked surprised. "Not seriously?"

"Yes, sir, I do," Schlesinger insisted. "As Dr. Mooers said, I want to do my part, too."

Beecher shook his head. "You're too young and inexperienced, Schlesinger. You wouldn't know how to take care of yourself."

"I've been taking care of myself for three years."

"Not scouting against the deadliest Indians in North America. I'm sorry, but the answer is no." He cut off Jack's protest with a sharp command: "Clear out of here, Stilwell."

As he left the barracks with Jack, young Schlesinger felt miserable. "I guess I'm just not meant for your kind of life," he said.

"Ah, we'll get you in the scouts yet, Slinger. They wouldn't take me the first time I tried, either. We'll ask Major Forsyth. You heard him tell the doctor he couldn't find enough men in Fort Hays to fill up his company. He'll want you."

Major Forsyth, however, took one look at Schlesinger's slender figure, asked him a few questions about his experiences, and shook his head negatively. When Jack promised to teach his young friend how to read Indian signs and other tricks of scouting, the major replied brusquely that there would be no time for that.

At the civilian mess tent, Jack refused to leave until he had exacted a promise from Schlesinger to meet him there early the next morning. "I'll be here," Schlesinger said. "And whether they take me or not, I've learned one thing about scouts. You never quit trying. I'll remember that, Jack."

* * *

Next morning, Schlesinger arrived an hour earlier than usual at the fort. He delivered his newspapers and was pleased to find his friend waiting for him at the mess tent.

"Skip breakfast for now, Slinger," Jack said hurriedly. "When I left the barracks, Sergeant McCall told me they still needed three good men. You'll be one of them if we get moving."

Schlesinger slung his saddlebag over his shoulder, and they started in a jog trot across the drillfield. As they entered the recruiting barracks the first man they met was Lieutenant Beecher. "We don't need any more boys," he said firmly. "We want tough old buffalo men."

Politely, Schlesinger pleaded for a fair trial. "I want to be a scout," he added. "How can I learn if I don't start sometime?"

"You have a point, boy," Beecher conceded. "And you've got pluck. Ask the major what he thinks. He just walked in behind you."

At first, Major Forsyth was reluctant, but he also was impressed with Schlesinger's sincerity and persistence. "Sergeant McCall, how many are now on our muster roll?"

"Forty-nine, sir. We just recruited a couple of sidebinders who wanted to sign on as 'Georgia' and 'Alabama,' and though I persuaded them to give me more presentable names I sincerely doubt if they are genuine."

"Galvanized Yankees?"

"I would guess so, sir."

"I hope those pure Confederate veterans we recruited don't kick up a ruckus with their galvanized brethren." Forsyth took out his pipe and tobacco. "Lieutenant Beecher, if you have no objection, we'll close our quota by adding to our truly cosmopolitan company a young Jewish lad from the city of New York by name of Sigmund Schlesinger."

"I waive all objections," Beecher replied.

At two o'clock that afternoon, Forsyth's Scouts, fifty strong, marched northwestward out of Fort Hays, with Lieutenant Beecher on the point as guide. The column was strung out loosely by twos, with the company's youngest members, Stilwell and Schlesinger, assigned to the rear to keep the four pack mules from straggling. Late in the day, Major Forsyth called a 30-minute halt to rest mounts, re-set saddles, and allow time for a cold lunch from the pack of cooked rations that each man had been warned must last him for seven days.

All afternoon, ridges of gray clouds obscured the sun and shortly after dark a drizzling rain began to fall. As neither Schlesinger nor Jack carried ponchos, they had to use their blankets for protection. Not until eleven o'clock that night did an order come down the column to make camp, and by that time both boys were thoroughly soaked.

Up ahead somebody was swinging a lantern. Sergeant McCall's deep voice sounded out of the dark night: "Dismount and form up by tens on me."

Schlesinger slid out of his saddle, stumbling in his weariness. Jack handed him the bridles of the first pair of mules. "Catch hold, Slinger. These ornery mules might take a notion to wander off."

After a great deal of confusion in the drizzle and darkness, the scouts arranged themselves in a ragged formation. McCall strode down the ranks, holding his lantern high, calling off names as he recognized faces. "Hurst, Murphy, Whitney, Gantt, Schlesinger. You men will take first guard, Gantt acting as sergeant. At 1:30 A.M. you will be relieved. Reveille at 4 A.M."

"Too bad," Jack whispered, "you drawing guard first night, Slinger."

With the drizzle blowing into his face, Schlesinger unsaddled and picketed his horse, and then reported to the circle of lantern light which served as headquarters. "You must be Schlesinger," a Southern voice drawled. A lean sun-bronzed face appeared in the dim light. "I'm Dick Gantt. We're going out now to set up our posts."

How Gantt could find his way in the blackness was a mystery to Schlesinger, but he kept close at his heels, the other guards following. "You take this spot," Gantt ordered softly. "Set yourself back under that old tree and keep your eyes along the creek. If you hear anything suspicious, holler. I'll be around."

In a few moments, the others were gone, treading softly through wet undergrowth. Schlesinger could hear nothing but the constant drip of moisture from the trees. After a while his eyes grew more accustomed to the darkness, and he could see the shape of the creek running silently below him. He found a place between two root outcroppings where he could brace his back. Then he placed his Spencer across his knees, drew his wet blankets over his head and shoulders and stared into the blackness, listening.

Soon the drizzle turned to rain, big drops pelting hard against the leaves above him. Gantt surprised him, appearing suddenly from nowhere. "Nasty night," he commented. "Not likely to be Indians about here, and even if they was they'd likely be holed up trying to keep dry like us."

"You were a soldier in the war, weren't you?" Schlesinger asked.

"Sure was. All four years of it. Then we lost."

"You were a Rebel, then."

"Yessirree. Seven of us in this company was Confederates." He hunkered down beside the boy, angling his hat forward so the rain would run off the wide brim.

"What's a Galvanized Yankee, Sergeant Gantt?"

"Call me Dick. We're not ranking in this outfit. A Galvanized Yankee? I reckon you mean old Georgia and Alabama. That pair was in a Union prison and took the oath to get out by joining the Union Army." He laughed quietly. "They suspect the rest of us Southerners look on them as traitors, but that's all in the past. If we'd been in their place we might've done the same—after all, they didn't fight us—they were sent out West here to fight hostile Indians." Gantt stood up, shaking the water off his leather coat. "Better be making my rounds."

The rain fell steadily, penetrating the sheltering tree, and Schlesinger's blankets clung clammily to his shoulders. Weariness from the long ride combined with the rhythm of the rain made him sleepy, but every time he was about to drowse off, Gantt appeared to give him a friendly word. Once he did close his eyes, and he was never certain whether he actually fell asleep. This time a rich Irish brogue startled him wide awake: "Relief guard!" A lantern dropped before his face. "You asleep?" the voice demanded hoarsely. Beyond the lantern was a ruddy face with a tremendous mustache that seemed to extend from ear to ear. "If you was in the Queen's Army, laddy boy, they'd be hanging you by the thumbs come morning."

"I was not asleep," Schlesinger replied.

"Then get along into your blankets. I was only giving you the gab." He held the lantern higher. "You're only a kid. What's your name?"

"Sigmund Schlesinger."

"Mine's Martin Burke."

6

martin burke

August 29–September 5

When he heard Sergeant McCall's whistle, Martin Burke circled the camp site and gathered in his guard detail. He was glad the rain had stopped, although judging from the gray dawnlight he doubted if there would be any morning sun to dry his soggy jeans. By the time he reached the camp, all the men were out of their wet blankets, as bedraggled a crew of human beings as he had ever seen.

Glancing once more at the heavy sky, Burke strode over to the picket line where his horse was standing with head down, its mane and tail beaded with raindrops. He dug his saddlebag out from under a heap of brush and found it almost dry. From it he took a folded saddle blanket and a muslin cloth. With a few quick strokes of the cloth he wiped most of the moisture from his horse's back, and then flung up the dry blanket. As he was fastening the saddle girth he noticed Schlesinger nearby, changing his wet shirt for a dry one.

"Well, now," Burke called to him, "I think I shall do the same."

He stripped quickly, shivering in the morning chill, and pulled on his only set of dry clothing—a sailor's blue uniform with bell-bottomed breeches. Several of the scouts coming up to saddle their mounts stared at him in wonderment. He grinned back at them. "I might as well give you chappies the whole show," he remarked cheerfully, and drew a pancake sailor hat out of his bag, clapped it upon his head, and danced a step or two of a hornpipe.

"Great day in the morning!" The comment was from Major Forsyth, who was standing with hands on hips, his head thrown back in mock amazement. "A sailor on the plains of Kansas! Burke, you told us you were in the British Army, not the Navy!"

Burke quickly stood to attention, saluting before he remembered that such military forms were not required of Forsyth's Scouts. "Sir, I won these blues in what you might call a game of chance at St. Louis. They're the only dry rigging I have."

Forsyth shook his head slowly. "I may rue the day I promised you scouts that you could wear what you pleased. Sergeant Mc-Call!"

McCall came up, leading his horse. "Yes, sir?"

"Lieutenant Beecher wants two men to ride as forward flankers this morning. He suggested Trudeau and that youngster, Stilwell."

"I'll pass the order along to them, sir." McCall repressed a smile when he looked at Burke's sailor uniform. "Burke, you take Stilwell's place with the pack mules. Schlesinger's bringing them in now."

After a hasty breakfast without coffee, the scouts marched out along a trail that followed the winding creek. Burke fell back in the rear, riding alongside Schlesinger. For the first hour the mules refused to keep a steady pace, but after the stubborn animals learned that they must move along to avoid proddings, they fell into the rhythm of the column.

"You still sleepy, lad?" Burke asked.

Schlesinger confessed that he could have spent another hour or more in his blankets. "I was just wondering," he added, "if that boy who took my newspaper deliveries has made his rounds yet."

"Sure, now, that's where I've seen your face before. Bringing papers into the Hays City hotel. I've been working out of there with Ben Holladay's teamsters. Maybe should've stayed, but this sort of life seemed more exciting."

Admitting that he had joined for the same reason, Schlesinger said that he would not mind his aching bones, his chafed skin, the hot sun, and cold rain if he could only learn something about scouting.

"My sentiments exactly, Slinger," Burke replied. "True enough I've seen service in India with a fine Staffordshire regiment. And I've soldiered with the New York Volunteers. But out here on the plains I'm as much a greenhorn as if I'd never suited myself in a uniform." He tugged thoughtfully at his long mustache. "It occurs to me that at first opportunity we should ask Lieutenant Beecher if he would mind our riding in advance tomorrow so that we may learn something about tracking and reading Indian signs."

That evening after the column had made an early camp on Saline River, Burke approached Beecher with his proposal, and to the Irishman's delight, the lieutenant readily agreed.

Next morning Burke and Schlesinger were relieved of duty with the pack mules and assigned as observers with Lieutenant Beecher. They rode out proudly under a clear sky, the air crisp and invigorating. Before noon Burke sighted the first buffalo herd, far off to the north. Beecher sent him back at a gallop to inform Major Forsyth that buffalo meat was available, and the major immediately dispatched a small hunting party with orders to kill only enough animals to supply fresh meat for the company.

Early that same afternoon, Beecher picked up the trail of an Indian party—the faint rain-washed marks of travois poles. "Not a war party because their women were along," he pointed out to Burke and Schlesinger. "And because the rain has fallen on them we know that the tracks are at least two days old."

Ordering his observers to remain where they were, Beecher rode back to confer with Major Forsyth. In half an hour he returned with two scouts, who were ordered forward at a trot to follow the Indian trail northward. Beecher turned his horse in the same direction, motioning for Burke and Schlesinger to fall in behind him.

The land soon became more broken, with dry gullies, and low ridges covered with scrubby brush. Occasionally Burke sighted the flankers, Stilwell and Trudeau, off to the right and left. Once he had to detour around a large prairie dog village, and was amused by the chirping barks of the animals as they plunged headlong into their holes. A band of antelope took shape suddenly out of a creek bottom, circled the advance riders and then vanished as if blown away over a rise in the plain.

"Personally I prefer antelope steak to buffalo," Beecher commented, "but Major Forsyth has ordered us not to fire any more weapons. Just in case there may be an Indian camp nearby, which I doubt."

"Why do you think there is no camp?" Burke asked politely.

"If there were a tepee village in ten miles of here, hunters would have been out among those buffalo and antelope herds. It takes a lot of meat to keep an Indian village fed." A sudden drumming of hoofbeats caused Beecher to pull his mount up short. Moments later a horseman appeared on a ridge just ahead, halting and waving his hat above his head. "It's Joe Lane," Beecher said. "He thinks he sees Indians."

The three urged their horses up the rise. "Signs of a big camp on the Solomon," Lane said matter-of-factly. "They may be leaving. Alderdice sighted animals moving off in the distance."

A mile ahead they found the other scout, Tom Alderdice, waiting in a patch of scrub oaks. He pointed toward a narrow ribbon of green and gray that was the Solomon River, and Beecher fixed his field glass on the spot. "They're animals all right," he said. "Antelope."

Alderdice grunted. "Don't tell me that's not a camp site down there."

It's a camp site and a big one," the lieutenant replied. "And fairly recent I should say. Let's have a look at it."

As they rode down the slope in a slow trot, Beecher signaled the flankers, Trudeau and Stilwell, to come in and join them.

During the following half hour, Burke and Schlesinger were interested observers as five experienced scouts read what was written on the site of the abandoned Cheyenne camp. After examining dead cooking fires, the condition of the grass and horse droppings, the scouts agreed that the Indians had been gone about a week. By counting the brown rings on the grass where tepees had stood they estimated that at least a thousand Cheyennes had been there, perhaps three hundred warriors. The horseshoe shape of the camp, with its opening toward the east indicated that they had gathered for a ceremony, probably a sun dance. Across a shallow ford in the river, they found a smaller camp, and then Pete Trudeau discovered a broken arrow shaft with Arapaho markings. "No women in the Arapaho camp," Trudeau declared. "All warriors." He also found something else, moccasin tracks with the toes pointed outward. "White man's feet," Trudeau insisted.

"There've been rumors of white renegades traveling with a band of raiding Arapahos," Beecher said.

By this time Major Forsyth had arrived with the column, and he listened carefully while Beecher told him what they had found. "Cheyenne and Arapaho," the lieutenant added. "They've been working themselves up to something. They moved westward, following game herds along the creek."

Forsyth was consulting his map. "Solomon River meanders out into dry forks somewhere north of Fort Wallace. Even though they've a week's start on us, we'll follow their trail."

For the first four days of September, Forsyth's Scouts moved steadily westward along the Solomon. Each morning, Martin Burke and his young friend, Schlesinger, rode out early with Lieutenant Beecher. Their saddle weariness vanished, their chafed skin healed, their sore muscles hardened. More important, by keeping their eyes and ears alert, they were absorbing a considerable store of scouting lore.

On September 4 rations began to run low, and Forsyth ordered hunters out to search for game. Grass was sparse on the upper Solomon, however, and the Indians moving ahead of them had taken what animals may have been there. For breakfast that day, Burke at his last scrap of bacon, and during the noon rest stop he finished his last piece of hard bread. When the column went into camp that night, Major Forsyth announced that they were forty miles from Fort Wallace and would try to reach that post on the morrow. He added that Jack Stilwell had managed to bag an antelope, and that volunteers were needed to prepare stew for the company.

Next morning Burke swallowed a cup of weak coffee, and joined Beecher and Schlesinger. Half an hour later, the Indian trail they had been following turned abruptly northward. "We'll wait here," the lieutenant said. When Forsyth arrived with the column, they held a hurried conference, and the general agreement was that the Indians were heading for the Republican River. "More grass up there," Trudeau said. "Plenty buffalo now."

"And a good base for raiding from," Forsyth added. "How many days are they ahead of us?"

Some of the scouts guessed three days, others four. Forsyth shook his head. "If we were not out of rations, if we had fresh horses—"

"They'll stay put a while," Beecher said, "when they make camp."

Trudeau agreed. "They stay through Drying Grass Moon, I think."

Forsyth stared for a minute at the Indian trail, and then said as if thinking aloud: "We'll make a forced march to Fort Wallace for rations and fresh mounts. Let's move out."

By noon the country was so level that there was little need for advance scouts or outriders. No rain had fallen there recently, and to avoid trailing in each other's dust, Forsyth ordered the company formed in a line front.

Martin Burke found himself riding between Schlesinger and Dick Gantt, one of the men who had been in the Confederate Army. Late in the afternoon as they rode steadily southward over the monotonous plain, Burke and Gantt were passing the time in light banter. Suddenly they noticed Beecher galloping forward ahead of the line.

"I reckon he's spotted something over that little rise ahead," Gantt drawled. A few moments later the scouts were far enough up the slope to see a camp of haymakers along a small stream off to the right. At the same time a shot echoed above the rumble of hoofbeats, and then a puff of smoke appeared above one of the haymakers' wagons. Beecher swung his mount about and came galloping back. From the camp behind him, twenty or more horse-men dashed into view, charging straight toward the scouts.

"Hostiles!" Gantt yelled, reaching for his carbine.

"Hold your fire!" Beecher was shouting. "They're not Indians. But they think *we* are!"

A single piercing yell broke over the noise of pounding hoofs, a wild "Haaa-ay-yooch," drawn out until its volume faded.

"That's a Rebel yell!" Gantt cried. He slung his carbine, megaphoned his hands and returned the call. In a minute the speed of the oncoming riders slackened; they approached in a slow trot, grinning at the scouts. "What in nation kind of outfit is this?" one of the haymakers demanded. "We took you for a bunch of Chey-enne raiders."

"Why, it's old Charley Christy," Gantt said.

There was a hasty reunion, most of the men recognizing old friends among the haymakers, but Major Forsyth cut it short. "Sun's near setting. Mount 'em up, Sergeant McCall, or we'll never make it to Fort Wallace by dark."

When they rode into the fort, lights were glowing in the bar-racks. A whiff of frying bacon made Martin Burke's mouth water, and he was thinking of food when a swinging lantern blocked the horseman ahead of him.

"Forsyth's Scouts?" somebody asked.

As Lieutenant Beecher answered the question affirmatively, two silhouettes came into view. "It's Dr. Mooers," Schlesinger said. "And Sharp Grover."

7

ABNER
(Sharp) Grover

September 6–10

The morning after the scouts rode into Fort Wallace, Sharp Grover walked down to the corral with Lieutenant Beecher to help select twenty pack mules for the expedition. "Tell you the truth, Fred," he said, "there're some mighty good riding mules in this string. If it was up to me I'd leave most of them mangy army cayuses your men rode in on and take mules instead."

"Agreed," Beecher replied. "We'll talk to the major about it. But you know how some of our wild young jaspers feel about riding mules. Hurts their pride."

Grover snorted. "Them as can't supply their own mounts will take what the Army gives 'em and like it." He squinted northward across the dry plain and made a vague gesture with one hand. "Out there, I'd feel a lot better forking a tough old mule than a spavined horse."

As soon as the quartermaster's herdsmen had driven the last of the twenty pack mules through a chute into a shed yard, Beecher glanced at the sun. "I'm overdue at headquarters. Would you mind going by the quartermaster warehouse? Make sure that my successor over there issues proper ropes, straps and rations to Sergeant McCall?"

"My pleasure."

They turned in opposite directions, Grover heading for one of the limestone buildings erected the year before under Beecher's supervision. When he reached the high front platform, the scout leaped nimbly upon it, and felt a sharp twinge in his shoulder muscles. He winced at the painful reminder of his unhealed bullet wound.

In the contrasting shadow of the warehouse interior, Grover saw Sergeant McCall with two young men, seated at a rough board table. They were sorting ammunition into mounds of forty rounds each. Behind them was a heap of pack saddles, leather straps, and coils of rope.

"Morning, Mr. Grover," McCall greeted him.

Sharp grunted a reply, and explained: "The lieutenant sent me by to inspect equipment." He turned the saddles over, examining them carefully, and tossed two or three to one side. "Rope's new," he said. "But most of these straps're too short for our big mules. Where do they keep the quantics, Sergeant?"

McCall stopped his counting. "Schlesinger brought them out." He glanced at a slender youth in faded brown jeans. "Where did you find the quantics, Schlesinger?"

"What's a quantic?" Schlesinger asked.

Grover almost smiled. He held up a length of rawhide. "Pack straps, boy."

Schlesinger arose from the bench. "They're back behind the rifle boxes, sir."

"Let's go have a look." Grover patted the boy on the shoulder. "You working for quartermaster?"

"No, sir," Schlesinger replied proudly. "I'm one of Forsyth's Scouts."

This time Grover had to choke back a guffaw. He started to say that when he caught little fish he threw them back in the stream, but thought better of it and held his tongue. If Fred Beecher had passed the lad in, then he must have spunk.

He followed the boy back to an old packing box beneath a dusty window. "Here they are, sir," Schlesinger said, and then added quickly: "I'm pretty green at scouting, Mr. Grover."

"I figgered so."

"But I'm willing to learn."

Grover pulled several straps from the box, measuring the lengths with his eye, feeling the leather. "Now, here's one, boy, long enough for a wide-backed mule. Feel how softlike it is. A good quantic has to be soaked in salt water to make it limber for pack tying. You match this one to about three dozen like it—make certain they all got hickory rollers in the wide ends, and bring 'em out front. I got to go back and tell that commissary lieutenant to pack ten days of rations."

Schlesinger's dark eyes blinked at him. "Thank you, Mr. Grover."

"Nothing, boy."

Grover met Beecher again at noon mess, and didn't like the news the lieutenant brought with him. "Sandy Forsyth's fit to be tied," Beecher began. "Telegram came into headquarters this morning asking for the scouts to march out to Bison Basin. Cheyennes raided the settlers' livestock, and they want their animals recovered and the Indians punished."

"Be a wild goose chase," Grover commented.

"Doubtless. But the governor of Kansas signed his name to that telegram, and even Sandy Forsyth couldn't tell *him* that. When the major politely replied that he was preparing an expedition to search out the Cheyennes' main camps, the governor suggested he split his command."

Grover almost choked on a chunk of beef stew. "Twenty-five men each way? Thunderation, Fred, we ought to have more'n the whole fifty if we should run into Roman Nose or Two Crows' bunch. What does Colonel Bankhead have to say?"

Beecher shook his head. "He's leaving it up to General Sheridan. It's my opinion that Little Phil isn't likely to turn down the governor's request."

"Confounded! If we don't pick up that trail again in another day or so, we'll be too late."

Beecher nodded dismally, and sifted a few grains of sugar into his tea. "The major wants the men notified that we won't be marching out in the morning. General Sheridan isn't due back at Fort Hays until late tomorrow, and Forsyth won't move until he hears from him."

For another forty-eight hours Forsyth held his scouts at Fort Wallace, and then at last orders came from Department headquarters to march to the relief of the Bison Basin settlers. Departure time was set for the next morning.

A few minutes before five o'clock on the morning of September 10, Sharp Grover strode into post headquarters where Forsyth and Beecher were meeting with Colonel Bankhead. They greeted him with "good mornings," but his only reply was a surly grunt.

Forsyth glanced at him. "We don't feel any happier about this than you do, Sharp. But orders are orders."

"I signed on to your outfit," Grover replied, "to find the hostiles' hideouts, not to round up settlers' livestock."

Bankhead frowned at him, then said: "You might pick up a good trail in the Basin."

"Mighty cold trail by the time we get there, Colonel, and just a bunch of wild bucks roaming, most likely. That trail the major was following on the Solomon included squaws and papooses. It would lead us to a big village for sure."

"That's out of the question now," Forsyth said.

A knock sounded on the door, and the headquarters sergeant held up a telegram. "Urgent, sir."

"Read it," Bankhead answered.

" 'Indians attacking freighters' train west of here. Send soldiers quick.' It's signed by the station master at Sheridan City."

Bankhead whistled. "That close?"

"Less than fifteen miles from here!" Forsyth cried.

"Telegraph the station master that help is on the way, Sergeant," the colonel ordered. As the door closed, he added: "But who can I send? I've only a depleted squad of cavalry left here to protect the post and perform courier duties."

Forsyth turned quickly. "How about my scouts?"

Leaning back in his chair, the colonel smiled faintly. "Mr. Grover wants a warm trail. All right, Sandy, saddle up your scouts, and let's see where this bunch of hostiles runs for cover."

"We're on our way," the major replied, and started for the door.

Bankhead called after him: "If the raiders' trail should go by the Basin, see what you can do to soothe those indignant settlers."

As Grover and Beecher fell in behind Forsyth, the lieutenant asked: "You feel better now, Sharp?"

"Some," the scout answered.

In less than two hours, Forsyth's Scouts were trotting their mounts alongside a scene of indescribable confusion. Overturned wagons, spilled packing boxes, dead mules and oxen were scattered along both sides of the wide road. A harassed band of drivers was attempting to restore order. The Denver-bound wagons had loaded at the Sheridan City railhead, and had not been in motion half an hour before the raiders struck. The Indians swept away most of the extra mules and had even stolen two oxwagons after killing the drivers.

The dead men lay beside the road, and Sharp Grover took time to dismount and pay his respects. Both men were Mexicans; he recognized neither of them, but felt a sudden rage against the Indians who had done the scalping. *It's high time the Army put a stop to these things,* he thought. *We've got to stop the raiders before they attack, root them out of their protected villages.*

Surgeon Mooers and the young lad, Schlesinger, who had helped him with the quantics both came alongside. "Not a pretty sight, boy," Grover said.

"No, sir. But if I'm to be a scout I must learn to look death in the face."

"You never get used to it," Dr. Mooers said.

Grover mounted quickly, and rode over to the scene of the attack. He made a wide swing to count the hoofprints of unshod Indian ponies; the tracks showed clearly in the marshy ground. In a minute or so, Major Forsyth joined him. "How many were there, Sharp?"

"I figger between twenty and twenty-five. They headed back north."

"Start tracking them. Lieutenant Beecher will maintain communication between you and the column."

Half an hour later, Grover sighted the stolen ox-wagons, overturned in a dry run. He urged his horse to a trot, and as he came nearer could see the partly butchered oxen beside the wagons. At the sudden sound of drumming hoofs, he brought up his rifle and with a quick jerk of his body swung around in his saddle. "I must be getting edgy," he said aloud. The approaching rider was Fred Beecher.

8

lieutenant
frederick Beecher

September 10–11

The scouts held to the steady pace set by Sharp Grover, and before sundown they covered twenty miles of the Cheyennes' trail. As dusk thickened, Lieutenant Beecher overtook Grover again and informed him that Major Forsyth was willing to keep moving as long as tracking was possible.

"Daylight's about run out," Grover said. "I been looking out for a camp site." He motioned toward a darkening line of brush and trees off to the west. "Water's there, and we'll be screened by the woods."

They waited until Forsyth came up with the column, and then swung leftward to the strip of timber. A small creek was running in a shallow ravine, with another grove of trees beyond. Beecher pulled his horse in beside the major's; they dismounted and began unsaddling beneath a tree. "Good camp site," Forsyth said. "I could use some hot coffee, but I suppose fires are out of the question."

"I wouldn't advise it, sir. The Indians probably stopped for the night on Beaver Creek, two or three hours' north."

"You think they know we're following them?"

"They've been moving pretty fast. They'll probably begin worrying about pursuers when their horses slow down tomorrow."

McCall was coming up the ravine slope. "All present and accounted for, sir."

"We'll build no fires here, Sergeant. Warn the men against making unnecessary noises, and have the guard kept within the woods line. We don't want to be seen or heard."

Beecher tried to ignore the dull pain in his legs. He stretched, yawned, and reached for his blanket roll. A minute later he was on his back, completely relaxed, looking up at the pale stars already showing in a cloudless sky.

He remembered nothing more until he felt McCall's hand touch his head. "Dawn's breaking," the sergeant said.

"So soon?" Beecher grumbled. His bad knee was throbbing and so stiff he could hardly make it to his saddlebag. He managed to swallow a piece of cold bacon, then took a pinch of tea leaves from a small canister and held it in his mouth until he could taste the bitter flavor.

A few minutes later he rode out with Grover. The sun's rim was on the horizon when they picked up the Cheyenne trail again and started north, with the head of the column fifty yards behind them. For the first half hour the trail was easy to follow; then they struck hard ground and the hoofmarks were almost indiscernible. Grover reined in his horse, and at about the same instant Beecher saw what the scout had seen. Two of the Cheyennes had turned off to the west.

Both men dismounted, following the curving tracks for a few yards, and then returned to their horses. "They doubled back, all right," Beecher said.

Less than half a mile farther on, he saw lying beside the trail a discarded bolt of cloth, stolen from the Denver-bound wagons. The hoofprints were more scattered now, indicating that the Cheyennes had been pushing their ponies faster. More tradegoods had been scuttled along the way—a tin of spices, a small keg of nails.

"They must've sighted our dust late yesterday," Beecher said.

Grover motioned toward a strip of willows just ahead, and signaled Beecher to scout to the left. They spread out, and by the time the column came up they had found signs of the Cheyennes' night camp.

Forsyth, still in his saddle, was frowning over his map. "Is this Beaver Creek?"

"No, sir," Beecher answered. "Only a small tributary."

"The Cheyennes were rather careless, camping no more than an hour from us."

"They had scouts in their rear. They didn't camp until they knew we were bedded down."

Forsyth shook his head in disgust. "I had hoped they wouldn't suspect our presence until we were closer to their village."

Grover was poking at a wooden box which had been broken open and its contents discarded as worthless by a disappointed Cheyenne. Metal lamp shades lay around it. "You can bet they'll try to give us the slip today, Major," he said.

Rising in his stirrups, Forsyth shouted back to McCall. "Let the men wet their horses' muzzles, Sergeant. Five minutes, no more." He turned back to Beecher and Grover. "You two do the best you can."

"We could use outriders now, sir," Beecher replied. "Four on each flank, at hundred-yard intervals."

He and Grover mounted and trotted their horses across the narrow sheet of water.

During the next hour the trail thinned gradually. Wherever the grass was poor and the earth hard-packed, Beecher became alert for tracks turning out. Singly and in pairs, the Cheyennes were dropping away from the main party. Occasionally one of the flankers would signal that he had picked up divergent hooftracks, but Beecher always waved the man ahead.

As they neared Beaver Creek the ground became sandy with many buffalo and antelope tracks. Although the Indian trail was fresh, it was difficult to follow. Beecher swung closer to Grover. "How many do you count left in the party, Sharp?"

"No more than a dozen. Maybe ten."

Patches of woods lay on either side, but the main ford of Beaver Creek was flat and open. They crossed it without wetting their stirrups, both men leaning forward to study the damp sandy bank beyond.

Sharp grunted, slid off his horse, peering carefully at the markings, sniffing the air. "They didn't cross," he said.

"Followed the stream," Beecher agreed.

He turned and rode back to meet Forsyth, informing him of the Cheyennes' ruse to throw them off the trail, and asking for six men to help search both banks of the creek. A mile upstream, a sharp-eyed scout named Jack Donovan found fresh tracks of eight horses leaving the creek. The Indians' deception had cost the scouts almost an hour, but Beecher and Grover doggedly resumed their tracking.

Again, singly and by twos the Cheyennes began dropping out. Along a rocky outcropping the tracks vanished altogether, and the two men dismounted. They were still searching vainly for sign when Forsyth arrived with the column. Beecher turned toward him, shrugging. "Disappeared," he explained.

"Dismount the men, Sergeant," Forsyth ordered, "and come forward."

The major sat down on a flat bench of rock. Beecher and Grover joined him and the three stared silently across the rolling country. *An artist,* Beecher thought, *would need only green and brown to paint this landscape.*

When McCall arrived, Forsyth took out his pipe and said: "All three of you know more plainscraft than I, but I am in command and must make the decisions. So let's see what we agree on." No one spoke while he lighted his pipe. "First, we're all agreed the Indians have seen us, they know we're following them, and they've scattered. Where do you think they're heading for, Fred?"

Beecher frowned slightly. "I don't know, sir. Most of them turned off west. That's all I can offer."

"Sharp?"

"As the lieutenant says, they seem to be edging west, but I reckon they'll turn north again."

"Do you think they'll rendezvous somewhere?"

Grover spread his hands. "Maybe so, maybe no. But sooner or later they'll all go on to their village."

"McCall?"

"From what I've seen, sir, I'm inclined to agree with Sharp. They're carrying booty and most likely will want to get it back to their village before they do any more raiding."

Beecher's voice was without enthusiasm: "I'll admit to that."

Relief showed on Forsyth's face. "Then it's settled. We'll keep going. From what you've told me, I'd judge in a northwesterly direction."

"Up the Beaver Creek bottoms," Grover replied. "They'll be wanting game along the way, and they know they'll find it on the Beaver."

Forsyth knocked his pipe out against the rock. "Agreed, Fred?"

"What else can we do?" Beecher tried to keep moroseness out of his voice, but his legs were throbbing with pain. Forsyth gave him a sharp glance, then ordered McCall to ready the column for marching. When Beecher arose, he almost collapsed, but managed to conceal his distress from the others. It was an effort for him to get back into his saddle.

They headed westward, with the curving line of the creek on their left. In places the grass was lush, the soil almost black, and there were enough trees to keep scouting parties busy searching for concealed hostiles.

After a short halt for nooning, they moved steadily onward. To avoid thinking of his physical pain, Beecher chewed on his dried tea leaves, tried to remember snatches of poems, and devised difficult mathematical problems in his head. But inevitably, against his will, his mind went back to that day at Gettysburg five years before. It seemed more like fifty years.

On that first day of battle there was no way of stopping the Confederates. They swept in like a flood, and when his regiment made a desperate charge, the Rebs came in on the flank. Beecher remembered his flagbearer tearing the regimental flag to pieces to keep it from the enemy. After they retreated to the ridge, only forty men were fit for battle, and because no one outranked him, Beecher took command. The next day was worse, the battlefield filled with boom-

*ing guns, chattering rifles and screeching shells. He closed his eyes
and it all came back, the scream of flying metal, the sudden shock
as something struck him and tumbled him backward, the wrench of
pain. He was sure that he had been cut in two. He lost consciousness
and when he awoke a surgeon told him his right kneecap was gone,
his leg shattered . . . .*

"You gone deaf, Lieutenant?" Grover's voice snarled into his
ear, and Beecher felt the pressure of the scout's horse against his
leg.

"Sorry." Beecher brushed his gauntleted hand across his eyes. "I
wasn't minding my business."

"The major's been yelling for us back there."

Forsyth was coming forward. "This creek's about run out," he
shouted. "If my map is correct there's no other water closer than a
day's ride north."

"You mean to go into camp?" Beecher asked.

"We'll camp, and send small details fanning out to see what they
can find. Have you seen any sign at all?"

"Nothing but a long dead campfire," Sharp answered.

The sun was only at midafternoon, but they made camp along
the headwaters of the creek. Beecher selected six patrols of six men
each, he and Grover leading two of them. For three miles out they
scoured the country north of the Beaver, and late in the afternoon
Dick Gantt's patrol found fresh tracks of four unshod ponies moving northward.

By the time the scouts reassembled in camp to make their reports, it was too late in the day to start tracking. Major Forsyth
advised the men to fill their canteens and turn in early; they would
have to be mounted and ready to move before next sunup.

Beecher was grateful for a chance to hobble down to the creek
and bathe his feet and legs. He found Dick Gantt there, soaking an
ankle in the shallow water. An ugly scar ran the length of his shin.

"Leg bothering you, Gantt?"

"Like a hot poker, Lieutenant," the Southerner replied in his
soft voice.

Beecher pulled off his boots and socks and started rolling up his
loose trousers. "War wound?"

"A Yankee Minié ball caught me at Gettysburg," Gantt explained. He stared at Beecher's legs. "Looks as if you got it worse than I did, sir."

Beecher laughed without humor. "We were on that same battlefield, Gantt."

Gantt shook his head. "I reckon we're living proof of what your General Sherman said about war."

Footsteps crashed in the brush behind them, and Beecher turned. Forsyth was there, a muslin towel slung over one shoulder. "Nobody hates war more than a soldier," said Major Forsyth.

9

MAJOR GEORGE
(SANDY) FORSYTH

When the scouts left Beaver Creek at dawn on September 12, Major Forsyth asked McCall to lead the column while he rode forward with Beecher and Grover. Forsyth was worried about Beecher. For two days the lieutenant had been dispirited, almost unsociable, and Forsyth decided to find out what was troubling him.

The sun quickly took the chill off the land, and the day showed promise of being another fine one. Birds were singing and white-rumped antelopes were frolicking on the plain as though it were springtime instead of almost autumn. To make a conversation, Forsyth said: "We've had good weather, at least."

Beecher replied with only an affirmative grunt, but Forsyth pressed him: "Something bothering you, Fred?"

Beecher's face flushed. "I suppose I have been a bit sullen, sir. Leg's paining me. Tried not to let on, but you've noticed, I see."

"I'm sorry." Forsyth remembered General Sheridan saying something about Beecher's bad leg wounds but that Grover and

Comstock had both insisted he was the only officer they wanted to scout under. "You were at Gettysburg, weren't you?"

"That's where I got the worst one."

"I served most of my time with Sheridan in the Shenandoah. Took four Rebel bullets myself. None bad."

"I didn't know."

"Oh, I ache here and there occasionally. Always reminds me I'm lucky to be alive."

Beecher pulled his horse abruptly aside, peering down at hoofmarks cutting into the trail. Off to the left, Grover raised an arm and called: "Now we're tracking five, Major."

"That's encouraging," Forsyth replied.

Beecher asked: "Weren't you with General Sheridan when he made that famous ride to Winchester?"

Forsyth was pleased that Beecher wanted to talk. "Yes, he chose two of his cavalry aides for that gallop—to rally the troops at Cedar Creek. But the day I'll remember most was at Appomattox Court House when General Lee surrendered. For the first and only time in the war, it seemed to me that all the misery we'd gone through had some meaning. At last it was all over." They talked about the war and men they had soldiered with, and exchanged anecdotes about military life until suddenly it was time for a noontime halt.

After reminding the scouts that they would probably find no more water that day, Forsyth unsaddled his horse, rationed himself a small piece of dried beef, took a swallow from his canteen, and then relaxed against a hummock of tall grass. A few feet away Beecher was sprawled with his head on his saddle. Forsyth rummaged in his bag until he found a small and badly worn book. "When I'm in the field I always carry a volume of Dickens," he explained. "Wonderful for taking one's mind off matters which can't be mended. Have you ever read *Oliver Twist*?"

Beecher's eyes were closed and he gave no indication that he had heard, but Forsyth began reading aloud and was still reading when McCall's shrill whistles signaled the noon halt was ended.

They marched forty miles that day, reaching water on Big Timber as the sun was setting.

At next dawn they were again in their saddles, and spent the morning following the trail along a series of small streams. After studying his map, Forsyth was convinced that the Indians were heading into Republican River country—stronghold of hostile Sioux and Cheyennes.

Most of the creeks were small, and seemed to be struggling for existence among quicksands. The land had become like a desert, with bare sandhills everywhere. Early in the afternoon, however, Sharp Grover reported that they were nearing a branch of the Republican, and when Forsyth raised his field glass he could see a green line of swamp willows to the north.

Two hours later as they were fording the stream, Beecher discovered an abandoned wickiup on the north bank. Forsyth turned aside to look at the crude shelter which had been made by bending willows to the ground, interlacing the branches, and covering the top with grass.

"Throw a blanket over that and a man could sleep cozy," Forsyth said.

"Two Cheyennes slept there last night," Beecher replied. "We're now trailing seven."

The trail turned west, following close to the river which flowed swiftly over a sandy bed, and was bordered by stands of elm, cottonwood and white oak. Beecher sent flankers out on both sides of the stream.

Late in the afternoon, Jack Donovan and Martin Burke came galloping in, their huge mustaches waving in the breeze, to report finding another Indian night camp. "How many were there?" Forsyth asked.

"Burke says three, I say two," Donovan replied.

"You Irishers better get together on your estimates," Forsyth remarked with a grin.

"No Irish ever agreed on anything, sir," Burke declared. But the veteran of the Queen's Army was vindicated a few minutes later when Sharp Grover reported that tracks of three more ponies had entered the trail.

They camped that night on another fork of the Republican, resuming pursuit at dawn in the same westerly direction. Almost hourly the trail grew more distinct, with additional hoofprints coming into it. At the noon halt, Forsyth asked Beecher and Grover how many Indians were now in the party. They agreed that there were probably twenty or twenty-five horsemen.

"The same raiders we started pursuing at Sheridan City?" Forsyth asked.

"Anybody's guess," Grover replied. "I'd wager some are the same."

"How old are the tracks?"

"Yesterday's, and if the runagates slowed down to do any hunting we may catch 'em today."

Forsyth shook his head. "We don't want to overtake them until they reach their village."

A faint hint of a smile showed on Grover's usually stolid face. "I figgered that. And if you're smart as I think you are, Major, you'll stay clear of their village, too."

Forsyth felt his temper rising, but held his tongue. He glanced at Beecher, who responded by suggesting that he and Grover move out a mile ahead of the column. During the afternoon, he added, if the main body of scouts marched at a slower pace, that would reduce the danger of alerting the Indians to their presence.

After consulting his map, Forsyth agreed to Beecher's recommendation. He was confident that even if the raiders should gain a few miles on them, another day's march would surely bring the scouts within reach of the hostiles' main camp.

Next morning, September 15, Forsyth ordered Sergeant McCall to inspect rations. McCall reported that coffee and salt were in good supply, but that most of the scouts had only enough hardtack and meat to last through another day.

For the first time on the march, Forsyth assembled the company in military ranks, gave the command to mount, then turned his horse to face them. "As most of you men undoubtedly know," he began, "we're in the heart of hostile country. Today or at least by tomorrow we should discover the location of their big village. If we succeed in this, some of you will be asked to ride faster than you've ever ridden before. The rest of us will have to maintain observation, possibly defend ourselves until regular troops arrive. You also know how low the rations in your saddlebags are. I'm asking you to make them last two more days. For another day or two we cannot risk disclosing our presence by firing weapons to kill any of the game which is in such abundance around us. Any questions?"

There were no questions, and they moved out in the chill dawn-light, still following the branch of the Republican. The land was now covered with great swards of buffalo grass. In some places the prairie was as smooth and green as moss, with occasional patches of a reddish grass that Forsyth had never seen before. The more luxuriant the country became, the broader the Indian trail grew until it became almost a beaten road with marks of travois poles several days old.

Around ten o'clock, Beecher came trotting back to report a split in the trail. "Up there it looks as if a regiment had passed over it," he said. He asked for a dozen volunteers, and sent them ranging far out toward a line of low hills on the north.

To keep from raising a dust cloud, Forsyth turned the column out of the trail onto the grass, and then increased the marching pace. He could sense an air of expectancy among the men. Had they been regular soldiers he would have passed a warning back to keep alert. With these seasoned plainsmen, he knew it was unnecessary.

At the midday halt, Beecher rejoined the column. He informed Forsyth that he had sent Jack Stilwell and two other men to scout the right fork of the trail. "Most of the lodgepole markings and dog tracks turned that way. About a week old."

Late that afternoon, Forsyth noticed dust swirls against the sun. He raised his field glass and counted four riders returning at a trot. In a few minutes he recognized Grover and Stilwell. The other two were Louis McLaughlin and the young lad, Sigmund Schlesinger. With a slap of his reins, Forsyth put his horse into a gallop and raced forward to meet them.

Grover pulled up beside Forsyth and reported: "The boys found your big village, Major. Trouble is, the hostiles already vamoosed."

"How long ago?" Forsyth demanded.

Stilwell answered: "Campfire ashes still warm, sir. This morning, maybe."

"They must have sighted our approach. How far away is this camp?"

"Two hours ride." Stilwell pointed to the north.

"Which way did they go?"

McLaughlin spoke up: "I scouted a short piece of their trail, Major. Into a canyon beyond their camp."

Forsyth glanced at the sun. "We can make it there before dark. Sharp, you round up Lieutenant Beecher and the other forward scouts, and try to catch up with us. Stilwell, you and McLaughlin move out as guides."

"I, too, sir?" Schlesinger asked.

"Sure, go ahead, lad. You're learning fast." Forsyth raised his arm and ordered the column to swing to the right. They were heading straight for a line of gray hills which in the slanting rays of the sun gradually changed to a hazy purple.

Near dusk they entered a draw that led into the wide mouth of a canyon, and there Stilwell pointed out the abandoned camp. Beside a large spring of clear water, Forsyth noted several rings of abandoned stakes where buffalo hides had recently been stretched to dry. It was obvious that the Indians had departed in some haste. "We'll make camp here," he told McCall.

A few minutes later, Grover, Beecher, and the other forward scouts rode in, and as soon as guards were posted, Forsyth asked the company to assemble around him. "Our Indians know exactly where we are," he said, "so tonight we'll have hot coffee." The men cheered. "Coffee is about all we have left, anyway," he added. "Stilwell and his scouting party tell me they counted some six hundred lodge circles on the ground around us. That would mean something like twice that many warriors, wouldn't it, Sharp?"

"Thousand at least," Grover replied.

"Twenty of them to one of us," a scout said. "We're asking for real trouble, pushing them like this, aren't we, Major?"

In the deepening twilight, the men's faces were indistinct so that Forsyth could recognize only those in the front ranks—hard-bitten plainsmen like Donovan, Trudeau, and the older Farley; adventurers like Burke, Gantt, and the anonymous Galvanized Yankees; mere boys like Schlesinger, Stilwell, and the younger Farley. "Every man of you was told before enlisting what the mission of this scouting company would be," he said firmly. "We shan't attack, but we will defend ourselves. Did you not enlist with me to fight Indians?"

"Aye, sir, we did that," declared Martin Burke. Someone else cried: "A thousand hostiles don't faze us, Major. If they're looking for a fight, we'll see they get one."

Later, Forsyth took a stroll with Grover around the borders of the camp to inspect outguard positions. Suddenly he heard a faint jingling of bells. He raised his head, scanning the horizon. Against the pale twilight sky on the rim of the low canyon appeared the silhouette of a mounted Indian. A second later the Indian vanished. Only the fading tinkle of bells assured Forsyth that he had not imagined the intruder.

"I heard them same bells the night Bill Comstock was killed," Grover said somberly. "That was Two Crows."

10

TWO CROWS

When Two Crows turned his pony away from the bluff, he struck his chest with his fingers and then flung his arm outward in a gesture of contempt toward the scouts' camp. Because the white men were burning their campfires openly, he had shown himself openly. Riding away, he shook his legs so the silver bells on his leggings could be heard clearly.

He let his pony set its own pace through prairie grass which in some places was as high as the animal's back. By the time he reached the crest of a low ridge, the stars were very bright in the sky. Spotted Wolf and the other Dog Soldiers were waiting there.

Without preliminaries, Spotted Wolf said: "We rode in all the directions, making a great round track. We found no sign of any bluecoat soldiers anywhere. The white men in the camp are the only ones in this country."

Two Crows dismounted. He felt tired and very hungry, and after he sat down he began chewing slowly on his last strip of pemmican. "It is strange there are only three bluecoats in that camp," he said. "Some of those men have lived with us in our villages in the north. Some are squawmen like the one who is called Sharp Grover."

"Their hearts have turned against our people," Spotted Wolf declared. "They would not have come this far unless they were looking for our villages."

"That is so," Two Crows agreed. "We must ride and warn our people. If we start now we will be there by the sun's rising."

"Our ponies are very tired," said Spotted Wolf.

"The white men's ponies are also tired. If we go now there will be plenty of time to protect the women and children." He stood up, stretched his arms and legs, and then leaped on his pony. The others mounted, and they rode off single file toward the north.

At daybreak they sighted several horses far off, moving parallel with them. Two Crows watched them for a while, then called to his companions: "They are Sioux warriors. Their village is not far from the one of our people." He urged his pony to a trot, the others following, and the Sioux slowed to let them catch up.

As he neared the Sioux party, Two Crows recognized one of them, a young brave named Running Elk. "Hoo-ee!" Two Crows shouted. "Are my Sioux friends riding to their village on the Arickaree?"

Running Elk replied that they had been riding hard for some time. Yesterday while they were hunting for antelope they had seen soldiers coming, and were hurrying now to warn the Sioux people.

"They are white scouts," Two Crows told him. "For two or three days we have been watching them. I think they are looking for our villages."

Within an hour they rode into the Sioux village, the Cheyennes accompanying Running Elk to the lodge of Pawnee Killer, and Oglala war leader. Pawnee Killer was in front of his tepee, brushing dried mud from the coat of one of his horses. He showed no surprise when Running Elk told him about the white men coming. "How many are they?" he asked.

Running Elk was not sure, but he said they raised much dust. Two Crows spoke up: "I counted them in their camp." He made the sign for fifty.

"They are not many," said Pawnee Killer. "We can stop them before they come to our village."

"Only three are bluecoat soldiers," Two Crows explained. "The others are buffalo men and fur hunters, and are very good at shooting."

Pawnee Killer's face was stern. "If the Cheyennes will join us, we will give them a good fight."

"The Cheyennes will join you," Two Crows promised. "We are going now across the river to warn our village. If there is fighting, Roman Nose will lead our warriors."

"Washte! Good, good." Pawnee Killer swept his hand out, to emphasize his approval.

Already the news was spreading in the Sioux village, and before Two Crows and his Dog Soldiers splashed across the shallow Arickaree, the camp was buzzing with excitement.

When he rode into the Cheyenne camp, Two Crows called to the first old man he saw sunning in front of a tepee: "Old man, go and cry through the camp that white enemies are coming. Tell all the warrior leaders to gather at the lodge of Tall Bull, chief of the Dog Soldier band."

Without a word the old man set off at a slow trot, his voice shrilling the warning and summons as he circled the ellipse of tepees. In a few minutes the warriors of the six Cheyenne fighting bands—the Fox, Bowstring, Buffalo Bull, Medicine Lance, Chief, and Dog—were gathering around Tall Bull's tepee. Two Crows and Spotted Wolf took turns telling what they had seen of the approaching enemies, and then Tall Bull added: "Our Sioux allies are preparing to ride out and fight them before they can come to our villages."

"Ay-ee!" cried Spotted Wolf. "Surely the Cheyenne people will fight at the sides of our friends the Sioux!"

By this time several Arapaho warriors who were camped nearby rode in to join the palaver. With them were two white men whose presence always made Two Crows uneasy. He watched the squawmen, wondering as he always did why they had chosen to live with the Indians. One was Nibsi, known by his own people as Black Jack; the other was Kansas, who also called himself John

Clybor. Kansas had been one of Yellow Hair Custer's bluecoat soldiers. After a fight on the Canadian River, an Arapaho woman had found him badly wounded and half-frozen on the prairie. She nursed him back to health, and Kansas had remained with the tribe. Kansas still carried his army bugle, and had taught the Arapaho warriors how to fight like the bluecoats, firing volleys and charging and re-forming at certain sounds of his blaring music.

During the palavering, Nibsi agreed with a few Cheyennes who wanted to send the women and children away and then wait for the white men to come and attack the village. But everyone knew that Nibsi was lazy and not a good fighter like Kansas. Two Crows was pleased to hear Kansas say that they should go and attack the enemies now, and drive them away before they came near the village.

"Kansas has spoken well," Two Crows said. "We will fight the white men in their way of fighting while Kansas makes them tremble with fear at the sound of his bugle."

"It will be so," Tall Bull agreed. "Let us drive in our horses from the prairie and prepare for the fighting."

In a moment the camp was swirling with excitement, the warriors hurrying off to find their fastest ponies and paint themselves for battle. Two Crows turned to Tall Bull. "I do not see Roman Nose anywhere. I see fighting men of the Medicine Lance band, but not their brave leader, Roman Nose."

"Have you not heard," Tall Bull replied, "that Roman Nose's medicine has been broken?"

Two Crows concealed his disappointment. "I shall go and counsel with him. Perhaps White Bull will help restore Roman Nose's medicine."

He found White Bull, the tribe's greatest medicine man, the one who had made the famous warbonnet which Roman Nose wore in every battle and which everyone knew protected him from flying bullets. White Bull shook his head sadly. He had spoken with Roman Nose that morning, but the warrior had received no sign that would assure him it was time to drive away his bad medicine.

"He must see the coming of the white men as a sign," Two Crows declared. "Let us go and make him understand."

Roman Nose was in his lodge, lying on a mat. He arose quickly and made room for his visitors to sit before the dying fire in the center of the tepee. His tepee furnishings were meager, for Roman Nose had never taken a wife; the water spirits had told him he must remain single and live only for the good of his people.

He was very tall, with a broad muscular chest. His black hair fell in braids over each shoulder, and his dark eyes held a fierce look until he smiled, showing strong teeth. "So the white men are sending scouts against us," he said quietly.

"Yes, they may come before the sun goes over," Two Crows replied.

"White Bull has told you that my medicine was broken?"

Two Crows nodded, and Roman Nose went on to explain: "When I visited the Sioux camp yesterday I ate bread which their women had lifted from the fire with an iron spoon. The Sioux did not know that my protective power is taken from me when I eat food taken out with anything of iron."

"They should have used a sharpened stick," White Bull said.

"You must start a ceremony," Two Crows suggested, "to restore your medicine."

Roman Nose shrugged. "I have looked for a sign all this day."

"Surely the white men coming with guns—" Two Crows hesitated, deferring to the medicine man who was supposed to know more about such things than a warrior.

"Roman Nose has not seen the invaders," White Bull said. "Yet if he has had a vision—"

"Each night in my sleep I see them on white ponies." He sighed. "Even so, the ceremonies to subdue my flesh and restore the power of protection will be long. Three days, four days—and you say the enemy may come before this day's sun goes over."

Two Crows restrained his impatience. "Our people are going with the Sioux to stop them before they reach our villages. I must hurry now and make preparations."

"Wait—" Roman Nose made the sign for sitting, and Two Crows remained where he was. "All summer our people have been gathering here for a great raid against the settlers. This time we must drive them away from our buffalo grounds forever. These white scouts you saw are like gnats worrying a great bull buffalo."

Two Crows listened, remembering all the palavers of that summer, how Roman Nose and the other leaders had planned for a great raid. At the coming of the full moon after the first frosts they would move eastward in bands of fifty to a hundred, taking their young women and boys to care for the plunder. They would burn all the settlers' houses, capture their horses, and then ride swiftly north to the Big Horn country where soldiers could not come because of the snow and cold.

"But first we must kill these gnats, as you call them," Two Crows interrupted sharply.

"With a thousand braves against fifty of them, they will run or die. Remember my counsel—do not fight them in the old way of our people, with every man fighting on his own, trying to count coups and show his bravery. Let all our warriors and their allies form in solid lines and ride over them in one charge. Not one white man will be left alive."

Two Crows nodded. "That has been decided by the soldier societies. The Arapaho squawman, Kansas, will blow his bugle for us."

"Go, then. It will be nothing." Roman Nose showed his teeth in a slow smile. "Now I must begin the ceremonies so my medicine will be strong again when the full moon comes. Then we will show the white men they can not take our buffalo land or run their iron horses across it."

The morning was growing late when Two Crows left Roman Nose's lodge. Everywhere around the camp, horses and men were swarming. At his father's tepee he was pleased to find that his sisters had brought in all his horses, and were busily assembling his battle trappings—his warbonnet, rifle, shield, lance, hand ax, and medicine pouch.

He went inside, changed his dusty buckskins for his finest clothing, rebraided his hair carefully, and then painted his face—the lower half with red ochre, his forehead with two circles of black to represent two crows. Into his beaded war bag he put an extra pair of moccasins, a mirror, and his medicine pouch, which contained sacred seeds, an owl feather, and a small yellow plume from his grandfather's pipe. Taking the bag and his short-barreled muzzle-loader, he went back outside to decide which of his six horses he would ride.

After examining the animals carefully, he told his sister to put his buffalo-hair war bridle on Bay-With-Star-On-Forehead. "He is the fastest and most sure of foot, but as he tires easily I will ride Gray-Speckled Horse until it is time for charging the enemy."

In a minute the horses were ready. Two Crows' father and his sisters came up to him in turn, placing their heads against his chest in farewells. He looped his war bag over his shoulders, mounted the gray, and rode off, leading Bay-With-Star-On-Forehead.

With Tall Bull and White Horse, he went on swiftly to the Sioux village. Several hundred warriors were scattered in bunches outside the tepee ring. Some were still making war preparations; others were coming in from hunts and scouts. The Cheyennes rode up to Pawnee Killer's lodge, and Tall Bull asked the war leader when the Sioux warriors would be ready.

"Many are ready now. When are the Cheyennes coming?"

"Two or three hundred will soon be here," Tall Bull replied. "That many more will come when runners bring in our hunting parties."

Not long afterward, a band of Sioux scouts came galloping in from the south. They had seen the white men, but said they were not moving toward the villages. "They ride straight toward the setting sun," the scout leader said.

Pawnee Killer smiled grimly. "They're following our old trail. When they come to the Arickaree they will know our villages are here to the north."

"If that is so," Two Crows said, "we will not fight them today but tomorrow."

"At the next sun's rising," Pawnee Killer declared. "By that time we can have a thousand Sioux and Cheyennes all around them."

"We will need some scouting parties to search out their night camp," Tall Bull suggested.

Two Crows spoke up eagerly: "I will go with eight or ten Dog Soldiers."

"Ride along the east side of the river," Pawnee Killer told him.
"I will send Running Elk along the west bank. When you know
where the soldiers are camped, light a signal fire. As soon as the
blaze is high, scatter it quickly."

Early that afternoon, Two Crows started out with his little band
of Dog Soldiers, riding in a southwesterly direction up the Arickaree. After a few miles, they began approaching each rise with
caution, a few warriors dismounting and running ahead through
the grass until they could see across to the next elevation. They
were in no hurry. Two Crows was especially careful with his led
pony, for he wanted it to be fresh for the morning fight.

Late in the day they sighted two white scouts off to the west,
riding in an opposite direction. Two Crows and his Dog Soldiers
watched from a plum thicket until the scouts made a wide circle
and turned back toward the southwest. "They are looking for fresh
trails," Spotted Wolf guessed.

"Let us go over behind that ridge," Two Crows replied.
Screened by low lines of hills that paralleled the Arickaree, they
moved on upstream, and not long before dark sighted the white
scouts less than a mile across the river. They were going into camp.
Here the stream was only a trickle in a sandy bed, with occasional
pools of still water. The white men had stopped near one of these
water-filled basins which lay below a small island. Horses and
mules were picketed close together, and sentinels were posted on
all sides as though they feared an attack.

"Soon it will be dark," Two Crows said. "We must gather grass
and twigs for a signal fire."

On a rocky ledge east of the ridge they collected a pile of dead
grass and then went in search of greasewood. After everything was
ready they rested on the ridge, watching the white scouts until
darkness fell. As soon as the stars were bright, Two Crows lighted
the dry grass. It flared up, burned without smoke for a minute, and
then spread to the greasewood. Black smoke poured skyward, and
then all the greasewood burst into a high brilliant flame.

"Stamp your moccasins on the embers," Two Crows said. When

this was done he told the others to mount and ride a short way back toward the villages. Then he crept up the ridge and looked toward the enemy camp, listening. He heard excited voices, probably the outer guards. One of them was shouting a cry of alarm.

11

MAJOR GEORGE (SANDY) FORSYTH

September 16–17

Major Forsyth was reclining against a saddlebag, pipe in his mouth, when he heard the call from the outer sentries. For a moment he saw the tip of the signal flame clearly above the hills to the east, and then it was gone.

Sharp Grover's voice drawled out of the darkness: "They're telling the warriors back in the village exactly where we are."

"I suppose there's nothing we can do about that now," Forsyth replied.

"Not a thing, Major, except sleep with one eye open and our Spencers in reach. Remember I told you before sundown that hostiles are thick all around us, and if they aim to fight us they'll do it just before next sunup."

Late that afternoon they had camped there on the grassy swale along the Arickaree, and after Grover and Beecher had combed the area they recommended that guards be doubled and that horses and mules be hobbled and picketed close together. Forsyth had issued an order to that effect, and he also ordered that all remaining rations—beans, bacon, and hardtack—be dumped into the cooking pots. From now on, he had told the scouts, they would have to live off what game they could find.

While this makeshift stew was cooking, he walked with Grover, Stilwell and Donovan across the dry bed of the Arickaree to a narrow island, a sandbar that ran parallel with the camp site. A slender cottonwood stood like a sentinel at the north end, and small alders and willows fringed the edges. A scattering of plum shrubs and grass as tall as a man covered most of the interior. Forsyth judged the island to be about a hundred yards long and fifty yards wide.

"Nothing here would stop a bullet," Grover commented. "But we could make a stand if we had to."

"I hope we don't have to," Forsyth replied. "If there is an attack I'm counting on our seven-shot Spencers to drive them off. They couldn't stand up against our withering fire."

"A small raiding party couldn't, no, sir." Grover gazed off into the twilight toward the north. "Trouble is, Roman Nose and Two Crows, they're learning to fight us different from the old way. If they come, they'll come in full force."

Returning to the camp, Forsyth had worked out a defense plan. Each man was to sleep with his boots on near his horse, and at the sound of any alarm he was to fall in, rifle ready, beside his mount and await orders.

As darkness fell they had eaten the last of their rations, swallowed a weak brew of coffee, and extinguished all fires. Forsyth had lighted his pipe with a coal, and was still talking with Grover and Beecher when the Indians' signal fire streaked the sky above the river. Grover's gloomy predictions depressed but did not alarm him. A few minutes after the signal flash he walked around the camp. The air was frosty already, and the men not on guard duty were rolled up in their blankets back to back for added warmth.

When Forsyth returned to his saddlebag, he could not sleep. He wished that he could read from his volume of Dickens, but any kind of light was out of the question. He lay for a long time listening to the snuffling of the horses and the snoring of some of the scouts, and the faraway wail of a coyote—that might or might not

be a coyote. Two or three times during the night he flung off his
blanket and made a slow circuit of the guards. None reported
seeing or hearing anything out of the ordinary.

Just before dawn he arose again. His carbine stock was damp,
and against his face he could feel a mist which had collected in the
valley, almost blotting out the stars. For a moment or so he stood
in the dark silence, orienting himself. He walked across the frosted
grass until his boots crunched in sandy gravel, and then he turned
downstream. A minute or so later a shape loomed against the graying sky.

"That you, Major?" He recognized Jack Donovan's voice, and
could almost see the scout's huge mustache. "Sky's lighting some
over that ridge."

As Forsyth turned to look, Donovan added quickly: "They
won't come that direction."

Forsyth fell in beside Donovan, who had turned back toward the
mule herd. Suddenly the scout stopped; he grasped Forsyth's arm,
halting him in mid-stride. "Listen, Major," he whispered.

Forsyth heard something like wind popping a guidon and then
saw a blur of motion. Both men cocked their Spencers, dropping
low in an effort to find the horizon line through the grayness.
Hoofbeats broke the silence, and a second later they saw the lead
horseman moving over the crest of a rise. He wore a feathered
headdress.

The two men fired simultaneously, and Forsyth bellowed an
alarm toward the camp: "Indians! Turn out! Indians!" He began
running backwards, firing again, counting the riders, and was relieved to see no more than a dozen. They were headed for the mule
herd, rattling dried hides to frighten them into a stampede. One
raider was beating on some kind of a drum. All of them were
yelling furiously, and it was light enough now to see that they had
cut away some of the mules and were swerving off out of range of
the guards.

Forsyth was gratified to find that the men in camp had followed
his orders like trained soldiers. They were standing beside their
mounts, each with his horse's lariat around his left arm, rifle

grasped in both hands. "Saddle up and stand to horse!" he shouted, and then noticed that two men were without horses.

He was giving them a tongue-lashing for their careless picketing when McCall appeared on the run to report that five mules had broken their lariats and been swept away by the raiders. "Add two horses," Forsyth replied harshly. He was pleased, however, at how quickly the scouts were bridling and saddling.

Meanwhile Lieutenant Beecher and the men guarding the pack mules had brought the animals in, herding them close behind the line of horses. "All supplies safe, including our extra ammunition," Beecher reported. "Indians panicked the whole bunch, and if Martin Burke had not held their ropes by brute strength more would have stampeded."

"I think I got one of the scoundrels," Burke said as Grover rode up on his horse. "One dead Sioux," Grover confirmed. He was scanning the horizon, his head turned to one side, listening. "The others are holed up in them rocks over there. Waiting for their brother tribesmen and the Cheyennes, I reckon."

Forsyth heard the sound then—a faint bugle call. He was wondering if there could be regular soldiers in the area, when the bugle call was followed by a rumble that was like thunder that did not fade away but increased in volume. Although the sun was not yet over the horizon, the light was much brighter now, and through drifting mists he could see hundreds of Indians charging up the valley, riding in a very broad front, the unshod hoofs of their ponies drumming on the grass. The bugle sounded again—the clear sharp notes of a cavalry charge.

"One of them white runagates with the Arapaho," Grover said. "Blowing that bugle!" He pulled his horse over beside Forsyth, his dark eyes bright as he looked expectantly at the major.

Forsyth calmly lifted his field glass, sweeping it along the charging line of warriors. Some wore warbonnets; others had braided their scalp locks with eagle feathers. They were armed with lances, rifles, bows and arrows. *They'll ride us down if we try to stand here,* he thought. He knew that every man in the command was awaiting his decision.

"To the island," he ordered, "and hitch horses in a circle! Sergeant McCall, lead out!"

"Your horse, sir!" Sigmund Schlesinger shouted. Forsyth turned and caught the reins from the boy, who stood waiting beside his own mount. "Move out, lad!" Forsyth shouted hoarsely. After a quick glance at the onrushing Indians, he stepped forward to give Burke and the mule-herders a hand. Burke was slapping one of the mules with his sailor hat, but the animal refused to budge. "Turn loose all mules except those carrying ammunition!" Forsyth ordered. "We'll drag them over by their ropes if we have to." In a matter of seconds they had those with ammunition packs in motion.

The Indians were no more than three hundred yards away now, still charging at a gallop. Forsyth jerked his horse's reins and started leading it on a run toward the island. Although half the scouts were already across the stream bed, the stragglers had abandoned their military formation. "Get across, boys!" he shouted. "You're moving like a flock of scared quail." He was surprised to find Jack Stilwell lagging at the rear.

"Sir!" Stilwell cried, "some of us would like to make a stand here under the river bank!" In a blur of motion, Forsyth recognized Harrington, Clark, Farley, Gantt—all excellent marksmen. He was raising his hand to wave them on to the island when Grover swung down from his horse. "They're right, Major! I'll join on with 'em. The hostiles can't see us down in that long grass bending over the bank, and when they slow their ponies for the drop-off, we'll have 'em clean in our sights and close as shaking hands."

Forsyth took the reins of Grover's horse and hurried on, plunging into the island brush just as the bugle sounded again. The Indians opened with a rattle of rifle fire that was as coordinated as any commander could expect from mounted troops in motion. Mixed with the firing was a crescendo of war cries—savage and exultant.

Beecher and McCall meanwhile had ordered the men to form their horses in a circle, tying them to saplings or bushes, and using them for cover. Some were already beginning to return the Indians' fire. Forsyth issued no orders, but took a position in the center of the circle where he could observe the action on all sides.

The charging Indians were at a momentary disadvantage, having to swing their front sharply leftward and then slow down at the eroded river bank. There it was that Grover and the others in the thick grass poured a deadly volley into their ranks at close range. Half a dozen painted warriors fell from their ponies, and the massed formation turned to wild disorder. From somewhere in the rear the bugler was blaring recall, but it was evident to Forsyth that the attackers had quickly reverted to their old way of fighting, every warrior for himself, riding in at high speed, circling, feinting, firing rifles and shooting arrows in wild recklessness.

In this flurry of disorganized attacks, the Indians hit a few of the scouts' horses; some animals broke their ties and fled, others fell to the ground. The scouts began unsaddling, using saddles and packs for cover. Forsyth now shouted his first order: "Start digging, boys! Dig with whatever you have—tin cups, plates, knives. Pack-and-saddle breastworks won't cover you. Work by twos. While one man digs, the other one keeps shooting." A bearded scout named Chance Whitney dropped down on his knees and began digging with his bare hands, pulling the knotted grass roots out of the sand by main force. Forsyth tossed him a knife.

"My horse took off with everything I own," Whitney said apologetically. "We ought've throwed our mounts down and tied their legs."

"Too late for that now," Forsyth answered. He bent over and slapped young Schlesinger on the back. "Two feet deep at least, lad, and long enough for you to lie in."

A dozen Indians charged almost to the horse line; the scouts responded with fire that was too hurried and too elevated as they swerved away. "Steady, boys, steady!" Forsyth cried. "Aim low. Don't throw away a shot. Don't shoot unless you see something to hit. Our lives depend on how we use our ammunition. Keep digging, keep digging!"

By this time the main body of Indians had formed into a circle, completely surrounding the island, gradually tightening the ring, concentrating fire upon the scouts' horses. On all sides the animals were rearing and plunging, screaming with pain, or falling dead in their tracks. Each circling Indian rode on the outer side of his pony, hanging by one hand and a loop of mane, firing under his mount's neck. They kept shooting continually, swinging away to reload, then rejoining the circle to fire again.

But the scouts were taking their toll of horseflesh, too, sending pony after pony tumbling, and sometimes bringing down the un-horsed riders before they could take cover. Gradually the circle broke, deflecting right and left as the warriors gathered up their dead and wounded and retreated out of range.

To Forsyth who was still learning the ways of Indian fighting, they seemed totally disorganized, but he suspected they would soon return. He urged the scouts to take advantage of the lull by digging their holes deeper, piling up banks of damp sand, and moving their dead animals into positions where they would serve as breastworks.

A stillness had fallen over the island, broken only by occasional taunting cries from the Indians and the steady scratching sounds of digging scouts. A voice whined behind Forsyth: "You don't know anything about Indians, Barney. If we get licked we'll be burned at the stake for sure." Someone else said: "He's telling you truth, Barney. Don't let's stay here and be shot down like dogs. Anybody want to try for the opposite bank with me?"

Forsyth spun around, his pistol out. "Stay where you are!" He kept his voice calm. "I'll shoot down any man tries it. Out of mercy. The surest way to a stake burning would be to leave this island."

Both Beecher and McCall had joined him in the center of the defense circle, their revolvers at ready. "Addle-headed fools," Beecher said. "Get back to your digging if you want to stay alive." The lieutenant's body tensed suddenly as he brought his weapon up, firing at a mounted Indian who had dashed out of the high grass and headed for the west bank.

A rifle shot from the bank knocked the warrior from his saddle, and then Forsyth saw Sharp Grover crawl out of his hiding place. After a quick glance around, the chief scout started running to-ward the island. When he reached the circle, he reported to Forsyth: "I had my eye on that one for a while, Major, and I figger there's more skulking around here in the grass. Thought you ought to know."

"I've noticed some of their horses coming over to join ours after they lost their riders."

"Some of them riders are still around, maybe listening to us right now. If we don't clean 'em off this sand bar, they'll crawl in on us. Give me a dozen men and we'll do the job."

Forsyth called for volunteers. With Grover leading, they spread out and disappeared in the grass to start a sweep toward the cottonwood at the north end of the island. A few shots sounded, and in less than five minutes they returned. One of the men, Pete Trudeau, was carrying a scalp. "Eight or ten others got away," he said apologetically.

Forsyth eyed the scalp with disgust. "Did you have to do that, Trudeau?"

"Old Pete was lucky he didn't lose his," Grover answered for him. "I knew that Sioux. His name was Bad Heart."

Martin Burke laughed and said: "Makes no difference whether his heart was good or bad. It's quit working now."

Shaking his head, Forsyth glanced to the west where the Indians appeared to be preparing for another charge. He ordered the scouts back to their rifle pits, and added: "Sharp, don't you think you'd better start digging a hole for yourself?"

The scout did not reply immediately. His head was angled; he was listening for something. "First thing we better do is call our sharpshooters in from the river bank," he said. "Hostiles know they're hid in there now, and the boys won't stand much chance in another attack." He walked to the horse line and whistled. A reply came back immediately and Grover motioned them to come over.

The seven men came out of their hiding place warily, crouching low against the bank, and then dashing for the island. Tom Murphy and George Culver came in first, just as a galloping band of Indians opened fire from the riverbed. The two scouts leaped over a downed horse, taking cover behind it. "Cheyennes!" Murphy yelled.

"Look out, Tom," McCall warned him. "That horse will kick; he's not dead."

"Rather be kicked by a horse than hit by a bullet," Murphy answered, and fired off a shot.

The Cheyennes wheeled away, some of them shaking long lances decorated with red cloth streamers. Beyond them Forsyth saw what he had dreaded, but expected. The main body of Indians was coming down from the high ground to join the new arrivals, their mounts advancing at a steady trot. At the same time the lance-bearing Cheyennes, as if vying with the warriors who had already tasted battle, swung back to charge straight across the river.

"Here they come again!" Sergeant McCall shouted.

Forsyth saw Culver rise up, and was about to warn him to get down when McCall leaped up to pull him down. A rattle of fire from the Cheyennes swept the west side of the circle, and both McCall and Culver hit the ground. As the attackers veered away, McCall sat up, gingerly feeling his neck. He reached for Culver, turning him over quickly. A bullet had smashed through Culver's forehead. "He's dead."

"And you're wounded, Sergeant," Forsyth said.

"Bullet grazed my neck." McCall tightened his bandanna against the bleeding wound and began reloading his carbine.

Grover meanwhile was trying to locate the other five sharp-shooters who had crossed from the river bank during the surprise attack and were somewhere in the brush outside the defense circle. He had crawled beyond the line of horses and was calling the men's names. In a minute or so, Jack Stilwell appeared, his auburn hair tangled with briars. "We've been trying to bring Mr. Farley in," he explained, "but he's too bad wounded. Maybe Hutch will want to be with his pa."

As Hudson Farley crawled out of his sand pit and started to follow Stilwell back through the brush, Gantt, Clark, and Harrington came in on their hands and knees. Frank Harrington was covered with blood from head to foot. "Harrington, you'd better see Surgeon—" Forsyth cut his words off, his attention fixed now upon the Indians who had halted across the river.

"Got an arrowhead over my left eye," Harrington said, "but I can still see good out of my right." He also was watching the Indians. "I reckon the surgeon and me are going to be too busy holding off them rascals to fool with it."

To Forsyth's surprise the Indians did not make another mounted charge. Suddenly as though by silent command, the mass of warriors divided, half of them turning downriver, the others upriver, gradually increasing pace to a gallop, and then one after another they leaped from their ponies and raced on foot toward both ends of the island.

Seconds later rifle fire was exploding from everywhere, filling the air with the *pict-pict-pict* sounds of bullets in flight. But not a living target was in range. "Major, you'd better get down," Dr. Mooers called repeatedly. Forsyth kneeled, shouted to his men to hold their fire until they saw something to shoot, and then he felt a bullet burn into the top of his right thigh. He glanced down; his trouser leg was darkening with blood. He fell forward deliberately, hugging the ground.

Mooers cried: "The major's been hit!"

"Just a scratch," Forsyth retorted.

"I'm going to widen my pit anyway," Mooers said. "To accommodate both of us. Some of you boys give me a hand."

So intense was the agony in his leg Forsyth could not speak for a moment, or he would have ordered the volunteer diggers back to their pits. The bullet must have struck a nerve, he thought, and then realized that although the enemy fire was growing heavier, most of it was blind shooting, too high to be effective. He held his breath until he could speak, then in a steady voice ordered one of the men in front of him to slow his rate of fire. "Be careful of your ammunition, boys, or this may be our last command." To ease the pain in his thigh he drew up his left leg. A second later he felt the jar of another bullet against the bone below his left knee. Mooers' bearded face suddenly appeared above him. "You've been shot again," the surgeon said accusingly; he and two other men began easing Forsyth into the surgeon's widened pit. He heard Grover's flat-toned drawl: "Varmints are getting our range, Major."

The rifle fire and the eerie yelling was almost continuous. From across the circle someone called: "Bill Wilson's been hit bad."

"I'll see to him," Mooers shouted back, "as soon as I can stop the major's bleeding."

After a moment the voice replied: "No use, Doc. Wilson's dead."

Inside the surgeon's sand pit, Forsyth managed to get into a sitting position with his back braced against one of the damp walls. While Mooers bandaged his lower leg—the shinbone was painfully shattered—Forsyth could see the last surviving horse tugging and straining at its lariat. A moment later a stream of arrows brought the animal down; its legs thrashed viciously as it added its hoarse gasps to the moans of the other dying horses.

From out of the tall grass came a comment in clear English: "There goes the last damned horse anyway."

"Who said that?" Forsyth demanded almost involuntarily.

Sharp Grover answered from the adjoining pit: "Likely enough their bugle player, Major. White runagates are with that Arapaho bunch."

Wincing from pain, Forsyth shifted his position so that he could scan the circle of defenders. "How many casualties, Surgeon?"

"Counting you, at least a dozen." Mooers began daubing antiseptic on Forsyth's thigh wound. "When they quiet down a little, we'll probe for that bullet."

Forsyth clamped his teeth together. Feeling pressure against his right leg, he reached down and found his watch. He was surprised to see that it was not yet ten o'clock. His head felt dangerously light and he knew that even though Mooers had slowed the flow of blood from his wounds he would have to exert a strong effort of will to remain conscious much longer.

Indians were everywhere around them now, mounted and dismounted. Not only were they on the thicketed island but they swarmed like locusts on the surrounding hills, the plain, and in the riverbed. Atop the bluff to the east, squaws with their papooses had gathered to watch the fighting, and above the noise of battle he could hear their weird chanting.

Out of the riverbed several mounted warriors made a bold attack, trying to overrun the scouts in their pits. Mooers reached for his carbine, took careful aim, and fired. "That rascal won't trouble us again," he said, and scarcely had uttered the words when Forsyth heard the sickening slap of metal against bone and saw the surgeon fall forward on the sand. "I'm hit," Mooers whispered. Forsyth was barely able to bend over to aid him. The wound was in the surgeon's forehead. He was still conscious but could neither speak nor move.

Raising his head to make sure the attack had been beaten off, Forsyth was startled to see Lieutenant Beecher standing in his pit, leaning upon his rifle as though it were a crutch. "Beecher! Lie down!" Instead of obeying, the lieutenant staggered across to Forsyth's pit. His eyes seemed glazed; he turned as if searching for something, then collapsed into the hole beside the surgeon. Blood stained the side of his ripped blouse. "I have my death wound this time, Major," he said softly.

"It can't be as bad as that, Beecher!"

Sharp Grover had crawled to the side of the pit, and stretched his long arms down to pull off Beecher's boots. "He always hated to wear boots," the scout said.

Beecher began mumbling incoherently. Forsyth clasped his shoulder gently, trying to understand what he was saying. Then, from the surgeon's bag he took cotton and bandages, and with Grover's help stanched Beecher's two wounds as best he could.

When this was done, Forsyth leaned back against the wall of the pit, breathing heavily. He could not be certain whether the firing was diminishing or whether his hearing along with his other senses was gradually failing. He forced himself to press his elbows against the wet earth, craning his head forward so that he could obtain a clear view of the field.

A screaming bullet thudded against his hat; he ducked, realizing instantly that the felt brim, doubled back for better vision, had saved his life. His fingers found the swelling on his skull; his head was already aching frightfully.

For the past several minutes he had been aware that someone was digging in the adjoining pit; then he saw sand crumbling over the unconscious forms of Beecher and Mooers. A hole opened, and he recognized the smudged and perspiring face of Sigmund Schlesinger. "Mr. Grover asked me to connect the pits, sir," the boy explained, and began lifting wet sand up with his hands to form an embankment.

Grover squeezed past the boy, balancing his carbine in one hand. "I figger we're going to be here a while, Major. Might as well make it easier for us to move around without presenting targets of ourselves." His eyes shifted briefly to the unconscious Beecher.

"I never expected the hostiles to be so well armed," Forsyth replied weakly.

"These are the same Indians that trapped Fetterman at Fort Phil Kearny and Caspar Collins at Platte Bridge," Grover replied. "They captured plenty of rifles at both places."

"And they seem to be well supplied with ammunition."

"Yep. Our only hope is they're running short now."

Forsyth had to fight away pain and weariness before he could speak again. "As soon as it's dark, I'll ask for volunteers to go for help."

"If we can last till dark. Must be eight or nine hundred Cheyenne, Sioux, and Arapaho out there. We haven't hurt 'em much yet."

Forsyth nodded. "Sharp, if I lose consciousness, I want you to take command. You know more about Indian fighting than McCall." He paused to take a deep breath. "Bring McCall here, so I can tell him."

Some time later, in spite of the continuous racket of firing and the distressing sounds of wounded men and dying horses, Forsyth drifted into an uneasy sleep. When he awoke again the sun was burning hot on his face and he felt an overpowering thirst. Using his elbows for support he pulled himself to an erect sitting position. His canteen was empty. From the sun he judged that it was past noon. The scouts were still in their pits, firing occasionally, but the only Indians in sight were scattered bands of mounted warriors who were keeping well out of range.

Schlesinger appeared in the connecting trench; he was carrying a tin cup in his hands. "Some of us have dug down to water, sir."

Forsyth thanked him and drank the tepid liquid slowly. He felt immensely refreshed.

Mooers began moaning piteously. "See if the surgeon can take a few swallows," Forsyth said.

Schlesinger shook his head. "He and the lieutenant are still unconscious, sir." Beecher's shoulders were lifting and falling with his hoarse breathing.

"I must have been gone out of the world myself for two or three hours," Forsyth said. "Have the hostiles made any more rushes against us?"

"No, sir, but Mr. Grover says they'll storm us again. He's down at the other end with Sergeant McCall."

"Has anybody made a count of our casualties?"

"I heard the sergeant say we'd lost two killed and seventeen are wounded."

As Grover had predicted, the Indians made another massive charge. They thundered across the stream bed, but the scouts' embankments gave ample protection and the hostile assault split apart.

At the height of the fighting, Forsyth managed to get his carbine balanced on the edge of his pit, lining his sights on a circling horseman who had darted in closer than the others. Suddenly he heard jingling bells, and he wondered if the sound came from that horseman. Just as he was about to squeeze his trigger, the Indian dropped behind his mount. Forsyth shifted his sights to the horse's shoulder, fired, and the animal stumbled, somersaulting its rider into the brush. Legging bells jingled again, and then were silent.

His strength gone, Forsyth sank back into the sand pit. He laughed mirthlessly, wondering if he had been lucky enough to bring down Two Crows.

12

two crows

Two Crows was down in the brush, his numbed shoulder beginning to ache from the fall. He removed his legging bells so they would not betray his position and then carefully hid them under a pile of dry reeds. Through the grass he could see his pony, Bay-With-Star-on-Forehead, lying quite still, eyes open but glazed in death. Truly, he thought, these white soldier scouts who had come with the bluecoat chief Forsyth were good shots!

Behind him he heard a rustling, and turned to discover his Dog Soldier brother, White Horse. "Are you bad wounded?" White Horse asked.

"It is nothing," Two Crows replied. "I grieve for my best pony."

White Horse held himself in a stooping position so that he would not make a target. "Your brother's son, White Thunder, has been killed. I took him to the women on the bluff."

Two Crows bowed his head. "Now I truly grieve. He was only a boy warrior."

"I will help you catch his pony," White Horse said, "so you can get back into the fighting."

Two Crows followed White Horse to where the latter had concealed his own mount. He leaped up behind and they galloped to the high thicket at the north end of the island. In a minute or so they found White Thunder's mustang. Gripping the lariat twisted around the pony's belly, Two Crows mounted and rode to join the Dog Soldiers who were reassembling along the east side of the river.

His eyes scanned the hills to the north. "Has no one seen any sign of Roman Nose?" he called. "I sent Spotted Wolf for him when the sun was there." He held his hands apart, fingers pointing skyward, to show how far the sun had moved.

"I do not think Roman Nose will come this day," Prairie Bear said.

"Whether he comes or not," Two Crows replied, "I must make one more charge to avenge White Thunder, the son of my brother. Will the Dog Soldiers follow me?"

Along the line of horsemen, a dozen red-streamered lances were lifted, and the eyes of all the warriors were fixed on Two Crows, awaiting his signal. He raised one hand, slapping it down hard on the mustang's shoulder, and they sprang into motion. "Hi-yi-yi!" Two Crows shouted. He brought his rifle up, firing at a head that showed briefly above a sand pit.

A second later his pony stumbled and he had to grip the lariat surcingle tightly and bend forward, catching the animal's mane between his teeth to avoid a spill. The mustang had stepped into one of the water holes that buffalos had used for a wallow; it was having difficulty pulling its legs from the muck. All around him Two Crows could hear bullets singing like bees, and then suddenly White Horse dashed between him and the island, zigzagging his mount expertly, drawing off the fire. At last, the mustang was free of the mud, and Two Crows signaled his brother warriors to withdraw. He was convinced now that the fire of the entrenched white scouts was too heavy for a mounted assault.

As soon as they were out of range of the bullets, Two Crows called the Dog Soldiers together and they rode to a plum grove where warriors of the other Cheyenne soldier societies were resting in the shade.

"You are a bunch of old women," he scolded. "Why do you not come and help the Dog Soldiers wipe out the invaders of our hunting grounds?"

"We are waiting for Roman Nose to come and lead us," Good Bear replied firmly. "The white men's bullets are too many for us to fight them in our old way."

Two Crows bent his head in assent. "It is true that Roman Nose has never lost a fight or been hit by a bullet, but his medicine is bad this day. We must keep up the fighting until he is ready to lead us."

Good Bear shrugged. "The Sioux, across the river, have stopped fighting."

Two Crows turned his head to one side, his face conveying disgust. "Their hearts are tired. Had the Sioux not allowed their foolish young men to raid the enemy's horses and warn them of attack, they would all be in the country of the dead. Had the Sioux waited until the Cheyenne people came here we could have killed all the white men before they could dig holes like prairie dogs on the island."

"The fighting has gone badly," Good Bear agreed.

Two Crows dismounted and began tying the mustang's bridle rope to a plum tree. "There is still a way," he said. "If the white scouts can dig holes and fight, the Cheyenne can dig holes and fight. We must make them keep firing their bullets until they have none left."

He persuaded fifty or more warriors of the other soldier societies to join with the Dog Soldiers, and then he led them on foot across the riverbed to a thicket of red-leaved willows at the north end of the island.

They crept through the willows until they reached the high grass, and then in a wild wave they rushed up close to the scouts' breastworks, firing arrows and bullets. When the scouts began returning fire, Two Crows shouted to his followers to fall on their bellies and dig holes in the sand. In a few minutes they had heaped up little shelters for themselves so that they were hidden from the men who were shooting at them only a few yards off.

Prairie Bear raised his head to shoot, and was killed instantly; then one of the Arapahos who had come with them made the same reckless mistake and was so badly wounded that Two Crows was sure he would die. "Let us fire our arrows over the sand heaps," he shouted to the others, "so that the white men cannot see us. Already this day they have killed more of us than there are of them."

After a while, Good Bear came crawling through the grass like a snake. "There is much excitement among the squaws on the bluff," he said.

"Go and see what is happening," Two Crows told him.

Good Bear stood up foolishly to run away, but he ran from side to side so that none of the bullets hit him. After a long time he returned, very excited.

"Roman Nose has come back with Spotted Wolf," he cried. "He is on top of the hill, sitting and looking at this island here."

Two Crows grunted with satisfaction. He passed the word for all the Cheyennes to slip away from their sand holes and assemble below the bluffs. He must go and counsel with Roman Nose.

13

ROMAN NOSE

September 17,
Late Afternoon

Roman Nose sat on the bluff watching the Cheyennes coming out of the red-leaved willows at the end of the island. Near him were Spotted Wolf and the medicine man, White Bull. They had drawn off to one side with the horses, leaving him alone to counsel with himself.

He did not like to see warriors of his proud people fighting on foot, but he knew that they had lost many horses and some of their best fighters, and were desperate for victory. Spotted Wolf had told him that the Sioux across the river and the Arapahos had suffered even more than the Cheyennes.

The western sun was warm against his face and he felt sleepy. He closed his eyes until he could see only a faint amber light, hoping for a vision. After a while he thought he saw many soldiers falling from the sky upside down, but there was snow in the sky and he knew that he was looking backward, seeing the great victory at Fort Phil Kearny in the Moon-When-the-Deer-Shed-Their-Horns. In that fight they had wiped out all of Fetterman's pony soldiers. There had been other victories, too, at Platte Bridge and Julesburg, and last summer at Fort Wallace they had given the bluecoats a good fight. But in those fights his medicine had been perfect. He could remember how bullets had sung all around him, but none could touch him because of his strong medicine and the protection of White Bull's magic warbonnet.

He sighed because he knew now there could be no visions for him on this day. When he opened his eyes he saw White Contrary and Two Crows riding up the slope toward him. "Well, here is Roman Nose," White Contrary called in his old man's voice. "Here is the warrior we depend on, sitting on this hill. He is the man that makes it easy for his men in any fight." White Contrary and Two Crows dismounted and sat down beside Roman Nose. "All the people fighting out there feel that they belong to you," White Contrary went on, "and they will do all that you tell them, and here you are sitting on this hill."

Roman Nose laughed quietly for a moment, and then said to Two Crows: "What the old man speaks is true."

"We know you have lost your medicine," Two Crows replied. "When your food was lifted with an iron tool—"

"Ay-ee." Roman Nose blew his breath with a whistling sound through his teeth. "It was White Bull who made the prophecy that bullets of bluecoat soldiers could never touch me when I go into battle with his sacred warbonnet and the power of his medicine. Let us talk with him."

White Bull was even older than White Contrary, and when he hobbled over to join the council it was plain that the joints of his bones were stiff and filled with pain.

"Have not the spirits told you," Roman Nose asked him harshly, "that I must be protected from the bullets of bluecoat soldiers?"

"That is true," the medicine man answered.

"But those men down there are not bluecoat soldiers. They are scourings of the white settlements—buffalo killers and wagon drivers and traders. They are not soldiers."

"They are good shots," Two Crows warned him. "They have

guns that shoot seven times without reloading, and they are dug into the earth like prairie dogs."

Roman Nose made a belittling gesture. "They are only a few." He flicked the fingers of both hands twice and said: "With the Sioux we are twenty to their one."

"The Sioux have withdrawn to lick their wounds," Two Crows said.

Roman Nose laughed. "Spotted Wolf has told me how the Sioux made a mighty charge right up to the island but their hearts were not strong enough to ride over the enemy."

"Yes, we could see them from the bluffs," Two Crows added quickly. "By the time we could join the fighting, the Sioux had moved into a circling wheel. None of us could get at the enemy."

"Our people have not yet learned how to fight the white men in their way. Many times I have talked of this with Crazy Horse, the greatest of the Oglala Sioux. He believes as I do—if our people are to hold our lands we must learn from the bluecoat soldiers to put all our best warriors together and fight all at one time." He sighed, stood up, and faced the sun, stretching his muscular arms. "Who will go and tell the Sioux that I am here to lead all our peoples in a mighty charge? Tell them I want only their best fighters. Tell them some will die, but I promise that all the enemy invaders will die."

"I will go," Two Crows said, and started toward the mustang.

With one hand, Roman Nose shielded his eyes against the sun and studied the island. The place where the white scouts were dug in was like a circular ant hill; the dead horses and the men in their sand pits looked very small and insignificant. Upstream the river made a gradual bend, and he decided that around the bend out of view of the enemy he would assemble his followers. When the warriors swept around the bend, massed compactly, the white scouts would tremble in their boots at the sight of such power! Surprise and terror would destroy their will to fight.

He turned to Spotted Wolf. "Go and tell the leaders of all the soldier societies to assemble around the bend of the river. Tell them we will attack from the south." He began loosening the rawhide ties of his war bag. "White Bull, we must go and prepare for battle."

White Bull arose, grimacing from the pain in his joints. "I shall ride with you in the charge."

"You are an old man."

"It is necessary that I ride with you. This day you will need all the power I can bring you from the spirits."

They mounted and rode behind the bluffs, taking the shortest route to the place of assembly above the bend in the Arickaree. Along the way Roman Nose halted and went into a little arroyo where he began making his preparations for battle. He removed his buckskin shirt and leggings so that he was naked except for his breechclout. From his war bag he took an elk-teeth necklace, a crimson silk sash, and a pair of battle moccasins. After winding the sash carefully around his waist, he covered his face with streaks of red and black war paint. When he had finished painting himself he went to his chestnut horse, whispering encouragements to it as he made secret markings on its shoulder to protect it from harm. He removed the thongs from his lance and fastened to it a red streamer which would help drive away the bad spirits. Last of all, he took the sacred warbonnet from its cylindrical rawhide case and unfolded it carefully. He straightened the numerous eagle feathers, placed it upon his head, and then remounted the chestnut. The feathers trailed behind him in all the colors of the rainbow.

Rejoining White Bull, he led the way silently on to the top of a hill from where he could see the shining sands of the river just below the bend. Most of the Cheyenne warriors were already there, and the Sioux were arriving in small parties.

For a minute or so Roman Nose held the chestnut there, looking across the country that had been his people's summer hunting ground for more moons than the oldest chiefs could remember. The sun was warm this day, but soon the moons of strong cold would come again, and the Cheyennes would be going back north to their winter lodges. He felt a strange sadness, knowing that he would never see the north country again, the country of high rocky hills and tall pines and clean singing rivers. His dream of a great raid to drive out the settlers was gone like the smoke of a dead campfire. But there was no other way. It was as White Contrary had said—the people felt they belonged to him and wanted him to show them how to punish the invaders who had come in search of their villages. He was the only one they would follow in the new way of fighting.

He turned his head, the feathers of his warbonnet fluttering, and said to White Bull: "If I go into this fight I shall certainly be killed." Without waiting for a reply, he kicked his moccasins against the horse's flanks and started down the hill.

When they reached the first stretch of level grass they met a party of Arapahos on foot. "We were few in number when we came into this fight," their spokesman said. "We have lost many of our best warriors charging these white scouts so that now we are too few to charge again, even though Roman Nose would lead us."

Roman Nose held himself straight, disdaining to make a reply.

"This man speaks for all of us," the white squawman, Nibsi, said. "There is much wailing among the women of our people. They gash themselves with knives and cut off their hair for their dead warriors."

"The Arapahos have no need to prove their bravery to me," Roman Nose replied. "Where is the adopted one of your people who calls himself Kansas?"

"Here." The bugler stepped forward, and Roman Nose smiled when he saw that the white man had painted his face so that it was dark like the skin of an Indian.

"I have thought of a plan," Roman Nose declared, "in which the Arapahos can help us when we make the charge. Divide yourselves and take positions as snipers on the two banks of the river. Have all your rifles and bows ready, and when Kansas blows his bugle you begin firing at the enemy so they cannot rise from their holes and fire at us when we ride down upon them."

"Roman Nose has spoken well," an Arapaho leader agreed. "We will do as he has said."

"Kansas will go to that low bluff jutting out there into the bend of the river," he continued. "When he sees me shake my rifle over my head like this, he will blow his bugle to attract the eyes of the enemy to our coming. When they see our mighty force their hearts will turn to water. We will let them have a good look at us, riding slowly. Then when I shake my rifle again, Kansas will blow for us to charge, and then the snipers along the two banks of the river will begin firing all at one time into the island."

"Ho-he!" the Arapahos shouted. "We will rub out our enemies before the sun goes over!" They began moving downstream toward the island, some taking the right bank, some the left.

With no further palavering, Roman Nose summoned the Cheyenne and Sioux warriors and after selecting the best marksmen for the front rank, he ordered them to form a line front of sixty horsemen, knee to knee, across the sand bed of the river. Behind these warriors he formed another solid line, and then another until he had eight lines, sixty men across. More than a hundred warriors still remained, but he assured them they would not be needed. "Go and join the Arapahos along the banks," he told them. "The more bullets we can send into the enemy from both sides the easier it will be for those who are charging."

After these men rode off reluctantly, he wheeled the chestnut and moved several yards in advance of the massed warriors. He looked upward to the sky which was filling with puffy white clouds against a deepening blue. "O, Great Spirit, pity me," he said aloud, and then lifted his rifle, twirling it lightly.

The bugle sounded sharp and clear, echoing from the bluffs, and Roman Nose waved his warriors forward. He held the chestnut to a walk until they were around the bend; then he urged it into a slow dancing trot. Glancing back, he gave a sharp barking command: "Ride close together, knee to knee!"

When he was sure they were all in view of the enemy, Roman Nose turned his horse and signaled a halt. "My heart is glad this day!" he shouted. "For my people and for our friends of the Sioux and Arapaho peoples. Though we have become few as leaves in the cold moons we are still brave warriors!" With a fluid motion of one naked arm, he gestured toward the bluffs where the women of all the tribes had brought their children to watch the fighting. "On those hills are the seeds of our peoples," he cried. "We must show them that no invaders can come and steal our lands or do us harm!" He turned his horse again and shook his fist at the island. A breeze fluttered the eagle feathers of his warbonnet.

With deliberate casualness he took his lance from its rawhide thongs. He pressed his knees up under his lariat surcingle so that if he was wounded or killed his horse could carry him off the field of battle. Drawing in a deep breath he uttered a war cry that rose to a taunting chant: "The men who dare follow me, come along with me!" He raised his rifle, spinning it contemptuously in his fingers.

A moment later the urgent notes of Kansas' bugle sounded the charge. Roman Nose slapped his quirt sharply against the chestnut's shoulder, and the horse broke first into a trot, then into a gallop. Behind him came the drumming of a thousand hooves and a high-pitched rising and falling clamor of war cries. He held his rifle in the hollow of his left arm, his fingers grasping mane and bridle, leaving his right hand free to flourish his lance to the women on the bluffs who were now chanting their war songs.

From both banks of the river, the snipers opened a rapid fire directly upon the island. After the first hail of bullets a hundred shining arrows streaked through the air, and then the firing began again.

Ahead, Roman Nose could see only grass beaten down by other attacks, dead horses, heaps of sand breastworks. There was no sign of the enemy.

Suddenly on his left a short-legged gray pony came abreast. Riding proudly as a young warrior was the medicine man, White Bull. He was stripped for battle, wearing only a breechclout and a small owl-feather cap. His naked legs were gnarled and swollen with knotty blue veins. He lifted one of his arms high, scattering yellow dust from a rawhide pouch. In his high voice he was singing earnestly to the Earthmaker.

Throwing his head back, Roman Nose sucked in his breath as though he were drinking deep of the blue sky; then he struck the palm of his hand across his mouth and screamed defiance at the bullets that were coming now from the island. Behind him he heard the cry, caught up and repeated by the warriors, and then it came back like an echo from the women on the bluffs. As it died away in the thunder of hooves, the women began singing their "strong heart" chant.

The island was very close now and its defenders were firing

desperately. Roman Nose raised his lance, waved it to drive away the power of the bullets, and hurled it defiantly toward the enemy.

In screaming volleys the bullets came—one, two, three, four. Off to his left Roman Nose saw White Bull fling his arms up; then the old medicine man fell from his horse. Five volleys! He knew there would be two more volleys before the men in the pits would have to reload. He used his quirt mercilessly on the chestnut's flanks and shoulders. Six volleys! Ahead of him over the rim of a sand breastwork he saw two enemy faces. As he squeezed his trigger he remembered a time long ago at a trading post when he had seen them before—an old buffalo hunter who called himself Pete Trudeau, and a curly-haired boy, Jack Stilwell.

14

jack stilwell

September 17–21

After Jack Stilwell rejoined the men on the island, he and Pete Trudeau and three other sharpshooters volunteered to move out to a position where they could obtain a more open field of fire upriver. Taking advantage of one of the lulls in the fighting, they crawled to the upper point of the island and there behind a thin screen of high grass began digging pits.

Within an hour the sharpshooters had dug two deep holes, piling sand breastworks around them. Stilwell and Trudeau were in the first pit, the other men occupying the second.

They made V-shaped notches in the breastworks so that when they braced themselves on their knees with carbine barrels pointing through the grass, they could command a wide angle of the riverbed.

Late in the afternoon there was a long pause in the fighting, and then suddenly a bugle call shattered the quietness. Jack was astonished at the size of the hostile force appearing around the bend in the river. Trudeau muttered something in French and began fumbling extra cartridges from his jacket pocket. "That's Roman Nose out there, boy," he said. "We're going to have real trouble now."

From the ring of pits behind them they could hear the other scouts talking excitedly. Then Sergeant McCall's voice rang out: "Hold your shots for close range, men! Wait for firing commands."

Again the bugle sounded and the mass of mounted warriors sprang forward in a charge. They came bounding onward, their horses kicking up a screen of sunlit dust. Jack raised his head just as a withering crossfire came from the Indian snipers concealed along the river banks. He dropped flat in the pit and rolled over, grinning ruefully at Trudeau. "You do that once more, boy," the old buffalo hunter growled, "and you won't never leave this island." A moment later arrows were swishing through the brush like dangerous snakes.

Jack crouched low, his knees well under him, rifle gripped in his hands. He set his sights on the warbonneted leader and awaited the command to fire. It came as Roman Nose's chestnut was about to leap upon the island: "Now!" Forty carbines fired in unison. On came the Indians, responding to the first volley with a taunting war whoop. After the jerk of the carbine stock against his shoulder, Jack held his breath until he heard McCall yell again: "Now!" This time horses and Indians fell, but others swept forward to take their places. Roman Nose began quirting his horse.

The third volley tore great gaps in the warriors' ranks, horses falling over each other. Roman Nose still came on at a swinging gallop, in a sort of weaving motion that so far had saved him from the fire of the forward sharpshooters. At the fourth volley his medicine man went down, but Roman Nose was so close now that Jack could see the warpaint on his face. Anticipating the fifth fire command, Jack raised himself slightly, sights set on the Cheyenne leader. In that split second, the chestnut faltered in loose sand, spun slightly, and Jack fired.

He never knew whether it was his bullet, or Trudeau's, or one of the other sharpshooters'. All he was sure of was that Roman Nose had been hit in the side or back, and had lost his reins. The chestnut lunged away, and the long-tailed warbonnet swept the sand. Roman Nose's legs loosened from under his lariat surcingle and he fell heavily against the grassy river bank. The sixth volley followed quickly, and the Indian charge broke apart in wild confusion.

Without a moment's hesitation, Jack began firing his revolver at the unhorsed warriors who had reached the island. They scattered in all directions, seeking cover. He calmly began reloading both his weapons.

"Any Indian as brave as that one," he said, glancing toward the motionless body of Roman Nose, "deserves better than being shot in the back."

Trudeau snorted. "Another wink of an eye and he'd had your scalp, boy."

The men in the defense circle had sprung to their feet to cheer wildly. "Down, men! Lie down!" It was Major Forsyth's voice, weak but clear. McCall repeated the order, and a moment later the forgotten snipers hidden along the banks fired a scorching fusillade into the island.

On both sides of the river the Cheyennes and Sioux were circling their horses, gradually collecting in small bands. Their leaders evidently were exhorting them to return to the attack. After a while most of them rode slowly up the river, disappearing around the bend. The sun was near the western horizon, and the white clouds were disappearing before a thickening gray scud.

Just before sunset the hostiles made one more half-hearted charge, but two or three well-spaced volleys from the scouts quickly sent them galloping out of range. "We've whipped 'em!" Jack cried.

"Wait till tomorrow to do your crowing," Trudeau replied. "They'll ring us in tonight and likely enough keep us here till they starve us out."

The sun was gone now. Trudeau squinted toward the right river bank, shifting his rifle slightly. Jack saw movement there; Roman Nose was still alive, pulling himself up the river bank by his arms, his legs trailing uselessly. "Don't shoot him in the back again, Pete."

"No, I won't do that, boy. Like as not he'll never fork a horse again anyhow."

For the first time since the morning attack, Jack felt a terrible weight of weariness. The twilight air was already cool, but humid with a smell of rain on the faint breeze. Night came slowly down.

"Trudeau! Stilwell!"

"Yea, McCall?"

"The major wants you men out there to report in."

They crawled back to the circle, where most of the scouts were gathered around Major Forsyth's pit. There was still light enough to distinguish faces, and Jack was glad to find that his friend Sig Schlesinger had survived without a scratch.

"I was lucky," Schlesinger said solemnly. "You, too, Jack. Lieutenant Beecher died a few minutes ago."

"He was one of the best, Lieutenant Beecher was." Jack rested his hand on Schlesinger's shoulder. "I talked you into joining this unlucky outfit, Slinger. I'm going to do my best to get you out alive."

"I volunteered, didn't I? Don't you think we stand a chance, Jack?"

"We beat 'em today. If we have to, we'll beat 'em again tomorrow."

"Well said, lad," Major Forsyth commented from his pit. He had been resting with his back against the sand, eyes closed, and Jack had thought he was asleep. "Gather in close," Forsyth continued. "Grover, McCall, come here by me. We'll try to assess our situation together." He took a deep breath and shifted his bandaged leg, clenching his teeth against the pain. "First, the problem of rations. For the time being we have a sufficiency all around us—our dead horses and mules—but the meat must be preserved by cooking or burying. Sharp Grover assures me that the Indians will trouble us no more until next daylight, and that if we use caution we can make fires in the deeper pits and cook over coals."

"Stay away from the fireglow," Grover warned, "and make no shadow targets for snipers out there on the river banks."

"Sergeant McCall, what's our present strength?"

McCall drew a folded paper from inside his blouse, but was unable to read from it in the dusky light. "I'll have to report as memory serves, sir. Lieutenant Beecher—God rest his soul—is no longer with us. Scouts Culver and Wilson both died bravely. Surgeon Mooers and Lewis Farley are unconscious. Scouts O'Donnell, Day, Davis, Tucker, Gantt, Clark, Armitage, Morton, and Violett suffered severe wounds. Scouts Harrington, Davenport, Haley, McLaughlin, and Hudson Farley—painful but not serious wounds. Adding the major, we have taken twenty casualties, leaving thirty-one men hale and hearty."

"You forgot yourself, did you not, Sergeant?"

"Only a scratch, sir."

"That neck wound of yours will be festering like a boil by morning. Make it thirty sound men, maybe ten others who can still take a hand in a hot fight. Forty Spencers can do a lot of damage, and Mr. Grover believes we'll see no more attacks as strong as the one led by Roman Nose."

Grover nodded agreement. "They've done their level best, Major. From now on it'll be prowling and skulking we'll have to watch out for."

"We have enough ammunition to deal with that," Forsyth said, "if we see to it that we make every shot count. Thanks to Martin Burke, our Irisher from the Queen's Army who first had the notion to dig deep, we have a well that supplies us with enough water to keep our canteens filled. On the debit side, our surgeon can no longer help us and we have no medical stores except what is in his bag, and most of those have been used up." He stopped suddenly, raising his head. "Is that rain I feel?"

"Only a drizzle," McCall answered.

Jack leaned back, letting the moisture cool his sunburned face. From the bluffs to the east, he could hear squaws beginning their wild dismal wailings for their dead warriors, and he shivered involuntarily.

Forsyth spoke again: "You can see I'm too badly disabled to stand or walk, but as your commander it is still my duty to give orders. We must strengthen and connect our rifle pits, take saddles off the dead horses and use them to help build up our parapets, dig out and fortify a place for our wounded, dress their wounds as best we can and cover them with blankets. We must deepen Burke's well. We must cut off a large quantity of steaks from the dead animals, cook and bury all that we do not immediately need. We must search all saddlebags for any ammunition that might be in them. Sergeant McCall will assign details."

McCall started to call off names, but Forsyth stopped him. "We have not yet considered our most serious problem. I purposely left it until the last." He paused for a moment to regain his breath. "You're all good plainsmen and you know the hostiles out there will try either to starve us out or wait until we run out of ammunition. Sharp, what are the chances of two men getting through to Fort Wallace for reinforcements?"

"Not good, Major. The Indians know we'll try to do that, and you can be sure they've drawn a close cordon around this island."

Without waiting for further comments, Forsyth asked quietly: "Any volunteers to try?"

Jack answered immediately, standing up as he did so. "Yes, sir, if you'll let me choose the man who goes with me."

Before the major could reply, other scouts were offering to go, and in a moment every man who was able to stand was on his feet volunteering for the journey.

"Being as I'm the chief scout," Grover said then in his slow drawl, "I'm the man should go to Fort Wallace."

"Out of the question, Sharp. You're second in command and are needed here." Forsyth turned toward Jack. "Stilwell spoke first."

"For what my opinion's worth," Grover insisted, "the boy's too young and inexperienced."

"Fred Beecher didn't think so," the major replied curtly. "Choose your partner, Stilwell."

"Pete Trudeau, sir, if he'll go."

Trudeau growled: "Of course I go with you, Jack. Why, you and me never fell into a scrape yet we could not get out of and I allow we can get out of this one."

"French Pete," someone said out of the darkness, "you're too old to make it. Let me take his place, Major."

"If the boy go, John Donovan," Trudeau retorted, "I go."

Forsyth interrupted: "We'd all like to go if we but could. In this case I think we can put our faith in Stilwell's youth and Trudeau's experienced maturity." He shifted his position in the sand pit, and was unable to suppress a groan. "Just before dark, Sharp and I tried to fix our location on my map. We believe Fort Wallace to be the closest point for relief, perhaps a little more than a hundred miles. A relief column, with wagons and ambulances, will have to return by way of Custer's Trail to the Republican, following the river to our position. At best we can expect no help for six or seven days—a full week's siege ahead of us. So—McCall, assign your details now. Get cooking fires going in the pits first. Stilwell and Trudeau will need a supply of horsemeat, and we want them started on their way as soon as possible."

In a few moments, the defense circle became a beehive of activity as details began carrying out Major Forsyth's orders. While some men dug in the sand to extend entrenchments, others butchered horses, cutting the meat into strips and laying them across small fires in the deeper pits. Trudeau took a pair of boots from one of his dead comrades, and cut off the tops to fashion them into moccasins. Jack found a ragged blanket, tore it apart, and wrapped his feet Indian style.

Their fires gave no direct light to the enemy, but the scouts carefully avoided the glow, and Jack found himself listening to every sound outside the circle. On the bluff, the Cheyennes' fires gleamed brightly, and death chants came in a monotonous rhythm broken by an occasional lamentation from a squaw.

When Jack completed his preparations for departure, Major Forsyth asked him to light a dry stick and hold it down into his pit so that he might see to write a message. By the flickering flame of the improvised torch, the major scribbled a note to Colonel Bankhead, explaining the predicament of the scouts and giving an approximate location of the besieged island.

Schlesinger appeared out of the darkness, carrying a tin plate heaped high with roasted horsemeat. "Is this enough to last you three or four days, Jack?"

"I could live for a week on that, Slinger." An aroma of broiled meat filled his nostrils, reminding him that he had not tasted food for twenty-four hours. He dropped the charred strips into his pack, then took out a piece and began chewing. It was covered with ashes on the outside and was raw on the inside, but he had no trouble swallowing it.

While he and Trudeau wrapped themselves in blankets so that in silhouette they would appear to be Indians, the others stopped their duties long enough to assemble for a farewell. "I have only this one map, Stilwell," the major said, "but you can make better use of it than we." He lifted himself on his elbows, and handed the map and message to Jack. "Boys, this is our last chance. If you can get to the fort and send us help, we can hold out a while."

They began shaking hands around, and John Donovan made a special point of singling out Trudeau. "I was only joking you about being an old man. You'll make it, Avalanche." Trudeau grunted and returned the friendly slap on the shoulders.

"Why do you call him Avalanche?" Forsyth asked.

"One time when we was scouting for the Army," Donovan explained, "a mule kicked Pete and we had to put him in an ambulance. In that French talk of his it sounded to us like he was calling it an avalanche."

The scouts laughed, and the sound eased the tension that Jack had felt building up inside him. He tucked the map and message into an inside pocket, tied his boots over his shoulders, and tightened his blanket. "Let's go, Pete."

He heard Major Forsyth's quiet-spoken "Good luck," and then he was in black darkness with Trudeau following soundlessly behind him. As soon as they were across the last pit, they started walking backwards to deceive any Indians who might pry into footprints at next daylight. The drizzle licked at their faces, but it thickened the darkness so that they were secure from observation in the open riverbed. When they reached the grassy bank they turned south, continuing to walk backwards in the sand for about a quarter of a mile.

They were now at the mouth of a shallow ravine where they had planned to leave the river, but Jack stopped suddenly, dropping to his knees. He could smell Indians. Trudeau moved against him, whispering a warning. A moment later they heard a rustling noise a few yards up the ravine. Without a sound they crawled away, circling southward again. A few minutes later a small mounted party emerged abruptly from a dry run that cut out of the bank, almost riding over them.

Jack dropped flat on the sand, straining his eyes against the blackness, not daring to breathe, fearful that his beating heart would reveal his presence. For the first time fear of capture gripped him, and he remembered all the tales he had heard of tortures and mutilations.

Trudeau's fingers touched his hand. In a crude sign language that long ago they had worked out for use in the dark, the old buffalo hunter urged him to leave the riverbed; the hostiles were using it for a night road. They crawled up over the bank and found themselves on a slope bare of everything except prickly pears. Jack's hands filled with needles; the sharp points penetrated even the blanket strips on his feet. He had to bite his tongue to keep from crying out.

Two or three times they changed directions to avoid prowling Indians. Once when they stopped, Trudeau whispered that he was certain the hostiles were searching for them; the Indians must have discovered some sign of their escape from the island.

Gradually the drizzle died away, a strong breeze brushing the sky partially clear so they could see a few dim stars, and almost before they realized it a faint dawnlight showed in the east. Aware that they were on a bald slope and visible for miles by daylight, they searched desperately for a hiding place. Just before sunrise they found a washout, overgrown with shrubs and grass. Moving carefully over rock outcroppings to avoid leaving footprints, they entered the hollow and after concealing themselves in the thickest grass, they made a small opening in the frost-blackened leaves of sunflowers that rimmed the washout. Jack could see for miles to the north; Indian war parties were scouting in all directions, riding single file, probably searching for him and Trudeau.

They resigned themselves to spending the day there, taking turns sleeping and standing watch. Soon after the sun rose they heard distant firing, and estimated that they had traveled no more than three or four miles from the island. They had lost valuable time dodging the alert hostiles, but at least they were through their lines now, and could move faster and farther the second night.

Around noontime a Cheyenne war party came within a hundred yards of the hollow, and Jack was certain that he recognized Two

Crows among them. The Indians circled the slope, looking for tracks. "Pete, if we left any sign, they'll be on us in a minute. We can't stop all of them before they overrun us."

Trudeau grunted, and bit off a chew of tobacco. "If it comes to that, boy, you save one cartridge for me. I'll save one for you."

A few minutes later the war party wheeled and trotted off to the northeast. Jack relaxed and began picking cactus needles from his hands and feet; later he ate some horse meat and drank sparingly from his canteen.

During the afternoon the sun was very hot, burning down upon them in the airless hollow. More firing came from the island, an occasional volley, and late in the afternoon for about half an hour there was a steady exchange of shots. At least they knew that their comrades were still holding out.

They were glad to see rain clouds gathering to bring an early twilight. As soon as darkness fell they moved out of the draw, heading southward. Twice they met bands of mounted Indians, but the sound of approaching hoofbeats warned them in time to conceal themselves. Light rain fell intermittently after midnight. At first dawnlight they reached a wide stream, but to their dismay they found they were within half a mile of one of the hostile villages. The only cover they could find was a strip of coarse grass between the river bank and a marsh. Once again they were blocked until nightfall, and with squaws and children roaming the area they were in greater danger of discovery than on the previous day.

Throughout the morning they watched squaws gathering dry willow sticks for fuel. In the afternoon a group of old men rode within thirty feet of them, halting to water their horses in the shallows. They talked in Sioux, and Jack understood enough to know they were discussing the fighting. They had lost many warriors, but they were sure they could starve out the white scouts in a few more days.

After the Sioux left, Jack drowsed while Trudeau kept watch. He was brought wide awake by a sudden keening that seemed to come from the very sky.

"Squaw mourning," Trudeau whispered. "They've been taking out their dead to put on scaffolds."

At first dark they waded the river, heading straight south for
Fort Wallace. A chill wind blew at their backs, dropping the temperature rapidly. To keep warm as well as gain miles, they alter-
nately jogged and walked, never halting longer than a minute or so
to regain their breath.

At dawn of the third day they were on a high rolling prairie, and
Jack guessed from his map that they were nearing the head of
Goose Creek. As there was no sign of Indians they decided to keep
moving, but at midmorning they sighted a small mounted party far
in the rear.

To avoid discovery they dropped to their hands and knees and
crawled into a clump of yellow weeds. The weeds had grown up
around a buffalo carcass at least a year old; the bleaching ribs were
still covered with bits of hide. They crawled inside the shell, and
lay with rifles ready, wondering if the Indians had seen them. The
wait seemed endless. A scattering of raindrops fell from the blus-
tering sky.

Trudeau complained of stomach cramps; he had filled his canteen from the river and suspected that the water had poisoned him.
More than an hour passed before the file of mounted Indians came
near them. "Cheyenne Dog Soldiers," Trudeau said. He groaned
softly from the pain in his stomach.

The Dog Soldiers had flankers out, and one of them rode very
near the buffalo carcass. He held his pony for several minutes,
waiting for the party to overtake him. He turned slowly in his
saddle, scanning the country in all directions. When he finally rode
away, Jack gave a great sigh of relief, then froze. "Pete!"

"Yeah?"

"Rattlesnake."

"I see him. He's cold. Wants our warmth."

"He's crawling toward us." The rattler was so close Jack could
have blasted it without aiming, but the Indians were only a few
hundred yards away. The snake continued crawling closer, and
when Jack moved slightly it went into a coil.

Trudeau moaned. "I think I die anyway."

With one hand, Jack searched in the side pocket of Trudeau's
jacket. "Your tobacco in there, Pete?" He found the plug of to-

bacco, and bit off a chew. He hated the taste, but chewed until he had a mouthful of brown juice. Taking careful aim, he spat at the rattler's head; in the next instant the snake scurried away into the weeds.

Trudeau laughed weakly. "Who taught you that trick, Jack?"

"Old trapper from up the Missouri."

"You miss that rattlesnake, he strike you."

Jack rinsed his mouth with water from his canteen, and said: "I was too scared to miss."

Before nightfall Trudeau became very ill, and sometimes seemed to be out of his head, groaning and muttering in French. When it was dark, Jack got him to his feet, and they followed the Indian trail to a creek. Trudeau drank thirstily, but immediately became sick again. He insisted that Jack leave him and go on to Fort Wallace.

"Eat some horsemeat," Jack replied. "If you can't keep it down, I'll go on."

The horsemeat stayed down, and after a few minutes Trudeau slung his pack on his back and said he was ready to go.

During the night, flakes of wet snow fell melting against their faces, and when dawn came the plain was shrouded in fog.

Late that morning they reached a hoof-marked trail that showed evidences of recent use. From his map, Jack estimated they were only twenty miles north of Fort Wallace. He wanted to break into a run, but Trudeau was too weak. He was debating silently whether he should risk leaving the old buffalo hunter alone on the road, when hoofbeats sounded from ahead. Jack had his rifle up when he saw the blue uniforms—two couriers riding like ghosts out of the fog.

"Jack Stilwell, put your carbine down!" The first horseman broke into a laugh, and Jack recognized his black shiny face, broken by a big tooth-filled grin. "Rube Waller!" he yelled.

The two Negro troopers were from the 10th Cavalry, bound from Fort Wallace with messages for Captain Louis Carpenter's command patrolling out of Lake Station. Jack unfolded his map, and found Lake Station. He hurriedly explained what had happened to Forsyth's Scouts, then showed Trooper Waller the X

which Major Forsyth had marked on the map to indicate the besieged island. "Tell Captain Carpenter what I told you and give
him this map. Tell him I said to gallop full speed toward that X.
Tell him the whole country in there is boiling with hostiles."

Trooper Waller nodded. "I'll sure tell him, Jack. You and old
Pete look mighty stove up."

"We've been dodging Roman Nose's hostiles for four days and
nights."

"Then I reckon me and my bunkie here better keep our eyes
peeled for Roman Nose."

Jack shook his head. "I think we finished Roman Nose. But
watch out for Two Crows."

15

TWO CROWS

September 17–18

When he saw Roman Nose go down in a jumble of wounded horses and warriors, Two Crows knew that the mighty charge had failed. Roman Nose had risked everything in spite of his bad medicine, but the spirits were without pity for him that day. Pressed on both sides by lunging ponies, Two Crows was swept toward the west bank of the riverbed. His dead nephew's mustang, which he was riding, took the bank in one leap, nostrils flaring, and Two Crows let the animal run for a few minutes to wear off its fear of the white men's whining bullets.

On the grassy flats he found Spotted Wolf, Cloud Chief, and some other Cheyennes riding in circles. They were waving their arms over their heads and uttering cries of grief. "Roman Nose and White Bull both are dead!" Spotted Wolf cried. "Our people have lost their mightiest warrior and his medicine man."

"Where are their bodies?" asked Two Crows.

Cloud Chief pulled his pony out of the circle. "Black Moon lifted White Bull from the sand and carried him away. I saw Weasel Bear riding bravely for Roman Nose, but the white men's bullets killed his horse. Weasel Bear had to run to save his life. Roman Nose fell into the grass on the island and surely is dead."

The Cheyennes gathered their mounts around Two Crows, who said: "We must make certain that our people have Roman Nose's body. We must not let the white men take his scalp and send his spirit wandering in darkness forever."

He led them back toward the river bank where they had seen Roman Nose fall, but the white men's firing was too strong and they withdrew out of range. Some leaders of the other soldier societies arrived then, and after a consultation with Pawnee Killer of the Sioux, it was decided that all the warriors would assemble again around the bend of the river. They would pretend to make another mighty charge, but at the first firing from the enemy they would scatter in all directions to gather up their dead and wounded, including Roman Nose.

In this charge, Two Crows and Spotted Wolf rode in the front rank, and although they chose the right moment to drop from their mounts they could not reach Roman Nose. They had to take cover in the grass only a few yards from where he lay, and there they waited for the sun to go down.

At first dusk they heard a faint brushing noise, a long-drawnout almost soundless sighing. Two Crows raised himself cautiously. "It's Roman Nose!" he whispered. "He's alive!" Disregarding the sharpshooters, he plunged through the grass and in a minute was reaching for Roman Nose's hands, helping him over the bank. Behind him in the deepening twilight, several other Cheyennes had appeared out of their hiding places.

There was still light enough to see that Roman Nose had been shot in the back just above the hips, a single bullet wound. He had lost much blood and was too weak to talk. Two Crows told him the Cheyenne medicine men would make him well again, but Roman Nose shook his head sadly. His eyes had lost all their fierceness.

"In a few minutes it will be dark," Two Crows said. "Let the young men strip themselves and carry Roman Nose to the squaws on the hills."

After a while the young braves formed a procession, the forward ones carrying their wounded leader on their shoulders, the others following in single file, beating on skin drums and chanting a death song.

"Why did you tell them to perform the death ceremonies?" Spotted Wolf asked.

For a minute or so Two Crows was silent. "Roman Nose spoke to me with his eyes," he said then. "He knows he has lost the power of his legs forever. If he lives he will sit all his days in a tepee like a helpless old woman. He has told himself to die."

They watched the slow-moving procession cross the river. When it vanished in the twilight, Two Crows went with Spotted Wolf and other Cheyenne leaders to meet with the Sioux. After a short discussion in the darkness they agreed to continue the siege of the island until the white scouts were all killed.

"We must make certain that none escape to go and bring blue-coat soldiers," Pawnee Killer said.

"None shall escape," declared Two Crows.

"The Sioux people are camped on the west bank," Pawnee Killer continued. "We will guard this side of the island."

"Then the Cheyennes will guard the east bank," Two Crows said.

After the parley ended, Two Crows and Spotted Wolf decided to go on the island and try to recover the bodies of two Dog Soldiers who had been killed there. One was Two Crows' nephew, White Thunder, and the other was Weasel Bear. Black Moon, Bear Feathers, and Cloud Chief offered to go with them.

"Be very careful when you go through the grass," Two Crows warned them. "It is dry and makes a crackling sound and the white men will shoot at any noise they hear in the dark." He led the way, slowly and cautiously. As they were creeping along, scattered out and going very slowly, two shots came from in front of them. A bullet cut across Bear Feathers' right shoulder, and he hugged the ground close to Two Crows. "Go back," Two Crows told him.

"No, it is only a flesh wound," Bear Feathers whispered. "I will stay here and keep watch for you." The others continued to creep up to the place where they believed Weasel Bear and White Thunder had been killed.

Although they moved as carefully as possible, two more shots came from the pit, close in front of them. One of the bullets hit the shield which Two Crows had tied on his back, and the force almost turned him over. The other bullet grazed Black Moon's shoulder. "It is nothing," he said. "Look hard in the darkness there. Do you see Weasel Bear and White Thunder lying in front of that rifle pit?"

"I see them," Two Crows answered.

Spotted Wolf who had been guarding the rear now came forward to help, but he moved the grass and the two white men in the pit fired again. One of the bullets hit Cloud Chief in the arm. Spotted Wolf crawled closer. "How much farther ahead are they?" he asked.

Two Crows replied: "They are right over there ahead of us, only a little way." After waiting a while, he gave a signal, very softly, and they crawled up fast through the grass. The white men shot twice again, but the bullets went over them.

Weasel Bear and White Thunder were lying almost side by side. Two Crows turned White Thunder over on his back. He was rigid in death.

"Look at Weasel Bear," Spotted Wolf whispered. "He is not dead. I can feel his body move; he is still breathing."

Two Crows bent over and whispered in his ear: "Are you still alive, Weasel Bear?"

"Yes, I am badly wounded; I cannot move."

"We are trying to get White Thunder away from here, and when we get him away we will come back and try to get you."

Weasel Bear answered slowly: "I am badly wounded through the hips and cannot move myself."

With a rope halter which Cloud Chief had brought along they passed a noose around the feet of White Thunder and pulled it tight. While the other men dragged White Thunder away, Two Crows and Spotted Wolf remained near Weasel Bear. A drizzling rain had begun falling.

Again the white men fired at sounds in the grass. They fired several times, but no one was hit. After White Thunder's body had been removed from the island, several other Cheyennes came to help rescue Weasel Bear. They moved very carefully along the trail that had been beaten down, and no more shots were fired at them.

Two Crows took the rope and got up to Weasel Bear. "We have come for you now," he whispered.

Weasel Bear said: "That is good. I am glad of it. I feel all right except that I cannot move my legs."

Two Crows looped the rope about Weasel Bear's feet, and they pulled him away slowly and carefully, making no sounds. At the river bank, some young warriors lifted him on their shoulders to carry him up the bluffs to the medicine men.

"I am very tired," Two Crows said. "I will sleep a little while, and then afterwards I will help with guarding the island." He rode his mustang into a ravine where he found a plum shrub to shelter him from the rain. He stretched out on the ground and fell asleep.

When he awoke it was very dark. The drizzle had stopped falling, and a strong wind blew against his face. He could hear the monotonous beat of drums and the wailing of mourners on the bluffs.

He mounted and rode out on the riverbed, searching for his friends. A few yards off he heard some Sioux arguing excitedly among themselves. One of them was Running Elk, who was down in the sand feeling for tracks in the darkness. "A young brave came and told me he was sure that one of the white scouts passed him in this dry river," Running Elk explained. "He said he smelled cooked meat and the odor of a white man."

Two Crows dismounted. "Have you found tracks?" he asked.

"Only a moccasin track and one whose feet were wrapped in blankets. They are going toward the island."

Two Crows felt the sand prints with his fingers. "These white enemies know our ways," he said. "They may have walked backwards to fool us."

"If this is so, we must find them," Running Elk said. "They will bring soldiers to fight us."

"I will call together the best trackers among the Dog Soldiers," Two Crows promised, and turned to mount the mustang. "Soon the sun will rise, and if white men are anywhere on the prairie we will find them."

As the sky brightened, Two Crows led his party far out, riding the crests of ridges and making a big circle. They scoured ravines and hollows, but found no sign of any white men.

They were two or three miles from the island when they heard firing in volleys. With a loud cry, Two Crows led the Dog Soldiers back in a fast gallop. By the time they reached the riverbed, the shooting had stopped. He saw Running Elk with a party of Sioux carrying dead and wounded on their ponies, and he rode over to find out what had happened.

Running Elk was angry and grieving at the same time. "It was some of our foolish young men," he explained. "When the sun rose they could see no sign of the white men on the island, no smoke, no sounds. They thought the white men had all escaped during the night. They rode up, about twenty of them, and dismounted recklessly, running forward to pick up the enemy's trail. They were surprised when the white men began shooting at them."

Two Crows sighed. "We cannot fight these men by rushing upon them," he said. "They are too deep in their holes. We must creep up on them through the grass in the old way, and make them shoot at us until all their powder is gone. Then we will kill them."

For most of that day, Two Crows fought in this way, tantalizing his enemies by rustling the grass near their pits, by showing himself for the wink of an eye, and dodging away. The white men, however, were sparing of their bullets, and would shoot only when a good target was offered. Too many of them knew all the tricks of the Indians. Two Crows fired several bullets at one of them, a young man whose head would bob out of his pit and then disappear. Two or three times the white scouts had cheered the young man for drawing fire. He was the one they called Slinger.

16

SIGMUND SCHLESINGER

September 18

A coyote howling far out on the prairie awakened Sigmund Schlesinger. Remembering suddenly where he was, he raised up and saw Martin Burke's friendly face grinning at him from an adjoining pit. "Quiet as a tomb, laddy boy," Burke remarked. "No redskins this day."

"Maybe they've gone," Schlesinger said.

"Don't lay any bets on that," a voice drawled from the opposite pit. Sharp Grover was peering out at the river where mist swirls lifted to the clearing sky. "Here comes a bunch of wild bucks now."

Schlesinger stood upright, his carbine ready, and in a minute saw about twenty Indians splashing their ponies through the shallows. They were moving at a slow trot, the leaders riding with heads high as if looking for something.

"Hot-headed young Sioux," Grover said. "They think we've vamoosed. Can't see us in these deep pits."

When the Indians reached the end of the island, about half of them dismounted and began searching the hard sand. To Schlesinger they appeared to be younger even than he, very young boys, but their faces and naked torsos were painted for battle.

Suddenly from across the ring of pits a single carbine shot rang out. Grover swore, then shouted: "Hold your fire till they get closer!" At the sound of firing, the mounted Sioux charged forward to screen those on foot. "Don't let them ride over us!" Grover warned. They came zigzagging in, but a rattle of carbines quickly scattered them.

"Got one!" Burke cried.

George Oakes, who shared Burke's pit, was standing up, rubbing his eyes. "They won't let a fellow get a wink of sleep," he complained.

"We would've cleaned 'em out," Grover declared, "if somebody hadn't got edgy and fired too soon."

Schlesinger reloaded his carbine and was reaching for his canteen when Sergeant McCall appeared in the connecting trench. "Have a good rest, Slinger?"

"If you can call two hours sleep a good rest, Sergeant."

McCall's face was lined with weariness, but he managed a smile. "You went off guard at three o'clock. I'm assigning you to help feed the wounded. The major says to heat some water. It'll have to substitute for coffee."

For the next hour Schlesinger was busy boiling water and warming strips of horsemeat. He selected the tenderest pieces for the wounded men who lay side by side in a deep wide pit. Major Forsyth, who was resting on a piece of canvas which Grover had stretched over a pole frame, refused to eat until the wounded scouts had been served. He obviously was in severe pain, but affected a jaunty air when Schlesinger offered him a canteen of hot water and a strip of meat. "Can't beat army rations, can you, Slinger?"

"Better than some of that tinned stuff they fed us in the contractor camps out of Hays, sir."

Forsyth's sudden laugh changed to a racking cough; he closed his eyes in a grimace of pain. "You have a way of looking at the brighter side, lad. I like that." He took a swallow of hot water. "Go ahead and eat. You haven't had a bite of breakfast, have you?"

Schlesinger began chewing on a strip of meat. Without salt it was almost tasteless, but at least it satisfied his hunger. "I hope my friend Jack Stilwell made it through with Trudeau," he said. "There's no way we can know, is there, for a time?"

Forsyth shifted his shoulders uneasily on the canvas. "No way at all, Slinger. If the hostiles caught them last night, I think they'd have let us know that in some fiendish way."

A bugle call sounded from across the river, bringing Forsyth suddenly upright, his head lifted high. "That blasted renegade bugler again!" he cried. The notes were repeated. Forsyth frowned, then shouted: "McCall! Grover!"

Head down and trailing his carbine, Grover darted out of a connecting trench. "Bunch of Cheyennes to the east, Major. They've put up a white flag."

Schlesinger turned in the direction of Grover's pointing finger. Five dismounted Cheyennes were standing on the river bank. A feather-bonneted warrior at center was holding a lance tipped with a fluttering white cloth. The bugle sounded three short notes and the five Indians moved forward into the dry riverbed.

"Shall we honor their truce flag?" Sergeant McCall asked.

Major Forsyth shook his head slowly. "I see no point in it."

McCall looked puzzled. "Perhaps they want to recover dead and wounded, sir."

A scoffing sound came from Grover's throat. "They've had all night to do that. All they want is to see how many of us are left alive in these pits."

Schlesinger watched the white flag moving closer. Evidently the five Indians were confident the scouts would not fire upon them.

"Order them to halt, Sergeant," Forsyth said calmly.

McCall leaped upon the rim of the pit, waving his arms and shouting at the warriors not to approach. From down the line, George Oakes' voice shrilled: "Tell 'em we're too old to be fooled by that trick, McCall."

Keeping his carbine balanced, Grover jumped nimbly up beside the sergeant and shouted several words in Cheyenne. The warriors pretended not to understand, and kept moving steadily forward; the lance bearer waved the white cloth from side to side.

"Schlesinger," Forsyth said firmly, "fire a warning shot over their heads!"

"Yes, sir." Schlesinger sighted on the white cloth, and then fired above it. The Cheyennes halted immediately. McCall and Grover dropped back into the pit.

Off to the right of the truce party, Schlesinger saw a single Indian appear on a sand knoll. "Two Crows!" he cried, swinging his carbine.

"Hold your fire," Grover said, and then megaphoned his hands, shouting in Cheyenne.

Still boldly exposing himself, Two Crows replied. When Grover answered in an insulting tone of voice, Two Crows suddenly disappeared, and the five warriors in the truce party scattered into the grass. A few shots were exchanged, and again quietness settled over the island.

"What did you say to him, Mr. Grover?" Schlesinger asked. Sharp's stern mouth twisted in a slight smile. "Two Crows said if we didn't honor his truce party they would charge us because they knew we had only a handful of cartridges. I told him to send on his bucks, that each man of us would give them a *hatful* of cartridges. I reckon he believed me."

Soon after Schlesinger returned to his pit, the hostiles renewed the fighting. They seldom showed themselves, but would fire suddenly from the brush or from long range positions.

From above a tree trunk that had been uprooted and left half-buried in the river channel, Schlesinger noticed a recurrent drift of blue powder smoke. "Hey, Burke," he called, "I think there's a sharpshooter behind that log."

"We'll see." The Irishman put his pancake sailor hat on the end of his carbine and lifted it slowly. Instead of a bullet, an arrow zipped out of the underbrush, sending the hat spinning. George Oakes laughed, but Burke valued his sailor hat highly and he began shouting insults at the Indians.

Determined to force the sharpshooter behind the uprooted tree to show himself, Schlesinger made a loophole in the sandy edge of his pit and carefully lined up his carbine on the target. Then instead of lifting his hat as Burke had done, he jumped high, exposing his head and shoulders for a second or two. After repeating this maneuver several times, he drew a shower of arrows from a group of Indians who were dug in behind cover of a knoll.

The arrows knocked down part of his parapet, and he scooped up a hatful of sand to repair it. This time a bullet screamed into the hill of sand. He ducked, squinted through his loophole, and saw blue smoke drifting again above the log. Once again he leaped, and this time he was certain he saw movement through the knotted roots at the end of the log. He emptied his carbine at the target.

George Oakes was yelling at him—something about saving his powder—and then Oakes let out a real yell: "Ow-eee!" A moment later Schlesinger heard Burke's raucous laughter. "Haw! Haw! Haw! Look at Oakes with a Cheyenne arrow stuck in his hind end!"

"Pull it out, you blasted Irisher!" Oakes shouted.

"It's only stuck in your pants," Burke said soothingly. "Barely scratched your skin."

The slight wounding of Oakes and the banter between him and Burke eased the tension of the morning. Not long afterward several Indians on the bluff mounted and began moving off, dragging travois behind the rear horses. Schlesinger asked Grover if they were leaving the fight.

"Mostly old men and women," the scout replied. "Carrying off wounded to their village. The bucks won't give up this fight yet awhile, boy."

By noon the sun was burning hot, and the slaughtered horses and mules that circled the pits began to swell and decompose. "If the Indians don't drive us out by tomorrow," Burke remarked, "the stench of dead animals will."

The afternoon passed slowly, with only an occasional scattered shot from the Indians. One by one they seemed to be leaving the island to gather on the hills along the east bank of the river. Grover watched them from his pit, his eyes scanning the darkening horizon. "Powwow," he said tersely. "They won't bother us no more today."

All through the late afternoon, Schlesinger had been hungrily observing a few ripened plums on a bush several yards from his pit. At dusk he crawled out cautiously, gathering handfuls of the fruit, filling his pockets.

When he returned George Oakes gave a loud cheer for him. Schlesinger offered Oakes a plum. "I gathered them for the wounded," he explained.

"My scratch hardly qualifies me." Oakes grinned. "Slinger, you may have been a greenhorn when you joined on with us," he added seriously, "but when the chips are down you're right there with us thick or thin."

The wounded men thanked Schlesinger heartily for the plums; that is, all except Dr. Mooers who was still delirious. Schlesinger bent down and placed a plum on the doctor's lips, then presented the remainder to Major Forsyth.

"Slinger," the major said in a voice grown husky from weariness, "I well remember how reluctant I was to sign you on as one of my scouts. I figured you to be a city tenderfooter from the East. Let me say to you now—and I shan't call you 'boy' or 'lad' ever again—you've proved yourself to be a gallant soldier among brave men."

Schlesinger turned away slightly so the major would not see how moved he was by the compliment; for a moment his throat was so choked he could barely say his thanks.

"Stay by me, Slinger," the major continued. "After I rest a bit, we'll have a talk."

Later on, just before darkness fell, Schlesinger took out a small notebook which he carried inside his shirt. He read his first diary entry, written on the day he joined the scouts: *Friday August 28, 1868. I put my name down for Scouting. Drawed horses.* He turned through the entries to a fresh page and began writing with a pencil stub: *Friday September 18, 1868. Indians made a charge on us at Day brake, but retreated. Kept shooting nearly all day. They put up a White Flag, left us at 9 o'clock in the evening.*

"What are you writing, Slinger?" Major Forsyth asked.

"My diary, sir."

"So you keep a diary? Well, do you know what I did this afternoon during lulls in the action—I began composing a poem in my head. Must write it down soon before I forget it." He took a deep breath, and shifted restlessly on the stretched canvas. "Perhaps I'll say it for you, Slinger."*

For a minute or so, Schlesinger waited patiently, then glanced at the major and saw that his eyes were closed, his face drawn with pain and exhaustion. He wondered how it must be to bear the awful burden of responsibility for men's lives—against pain of wounds, lack of sleep, and overwhelming odds—like Major Sandy Forsyth.

* Major Forsyth later published the poem in a book written about his Army life:

> When the foe charged on the breastworks
>   With the madness of despair,
> And the bravest souls were tested,
>   The little Jew was there.
>
> When the weary dozed on duty
>   Or the wounded needed care,
> When another shot was called for,
>   The little Jew was there.
>
> With the festering dead around them,
>   Shedding poison in the air,
> When the crippled chieftain ordered,
>   The little Jew was there.

17

MAJOR GEORGE (SANDY) FORSYTH

September 18–19

Major Forsyth slept fitfully through the night of the 18th. At times
the pain in his right thigh was agonizing. He could hear the faint
breathing of Dr. Mooers, who still lay unconscious opposite him.
Occasionally the surgeon's foot would move against his, as though
reaching out to make certain that someone was still there.

Once during the darkest and quietest hour of the night Forsyth
heard geese honking overhead, heading south, and he guessed their
flight heralded a blast of cold weather. The thought made him
shiver involuntarily, and he drew his blanket closer until the heat
of his fevered body made him throw it off again.

He was drifting into what he thought was a coma when a rattle
of carbine fire brought him wide awake. His eyes blinked against
sunrise. Grover was in the next pit, reloading his weapon.

"They're not trying very hard this morning, Major," the scout
said. "Just testing us, to see if we still have ammunition left."

When Forsyth sat up, he was shocked at how swollen his right
leg was, how bright red the skin was through his ripped trouser leg.

He touched the swelling on his inner thigh where the bullet was still imbedded. It was the size of an egg, pressing against an artery. The bullet would have to come out soon.

A few minutes later, Schlesinger's cheerful face appeared in the trench; he offered the major a strip of horsemeat and a tin cup steaming with hot water. "I'm afraid the meat's gone reasty, sir," the boy said apologetically.

Forsyth sniffed the charred strip, tasted it gingerly. It was beginning to smell of decay, but he chewed steadily, washing it down with hot water. "If we only had salt, we could keep it for days yet." He paused and looked out across the sandy waste of the river. "I wonder . . . Is Sergeant McCall nearby?"

"Yes, sir," McCall answered for himself. He had been hunkered down in Grover's pit, faithfully totaling up his morning report on a regulation army form.

"Any change in our casualties?" the major asked.

"One more yesterday. Slight. George Oakes."

"We're doing better. I think our chief concern now is rations. Starvation may become more of an enemy than the hostiles out there."

McCall agreed. "Our meat won't keep long in these hot days, for sure."

"Was there any gunpowder on the pack mules Burke brought over?"

"A couple of small kegs."

"How is our cartridge supply holding?"

"At the rate we fired yesterday, they'll last another five or six days."

"Good. Assign a couple of men to break open a keg of gunpowder and sprinkle some of it on the soundest cuts of meat we have left. The saltpetre will preserve it and give it some flavor."

McCall nodded. "I should have thought of that, sir."

"No matter. Another thing we can do when it comes dark again is to hang thin strips of meat on the taller bushes where the sun will dry it. The Indians do that."

"Yes, sir. I noticed Lew McLaughlin put meat shavings out on his gum blanket in the sun yesterday and it dried nicely."

Forsyth sipped the last of the hot water and tried to fight away the throbbing torture of his leg. "We must guard against scurvy, too. Schlesinger brought in a few plums at dusk yesterday. Assign a detail to gather more this evening. Ration them out so every man has a few."

Grover, who had been listening, now spoke up. "Plenty of prickly pears around here, too, Major. I recollect one time Bill Comstock and me lived a week on prickly pears. We boiled 'em down to a sirup. Needles bothered us some, but they kept us alive."

"We'll give them a try. But warn the men—" He cut his words off, and bent over to squeeze at his leg.

"That leg is tormenting you, I reckon, Major." Grover kneeled to examine the unbandaged wound. "Bullet ought to come out, for sure. If it wasn't for my bad shoulder, I'd have a try myself, but my hand's not steady enough. A knife slip there and you'd bleed to death."

Forsyth glanced at Dr. Mooers, who lay motionless except for his irregularly twitching foot. The plum that Schlesinger had placed on his lips the day before had rolled down into his beard. "If only the surgeon—"

"How about Al Pliley?" McCall suggested. "He's some kind of a doc, I hear."

They called Pliley, and a lean, haggard man came in hesitantly through the trench. Forsyth greeted him with forced heartiness in his voice: "They tell me you're some kind of a doctor, Al."

"No, sir, I'm no doctor. I worked a little while for a horse veterinarian, that's all, Major."

"You see this bullet in my upper thigh? It's got to come out."

Pliley studied the festering wound and the swollen lump beside it. "You'd ought to wait till a real surgeon can do the cutting. Bullet's buried itself in by what they call the femoral artery—"

Forsyth was swept by sudden peevish anger. "Damn you, Pliley, if you know the name of the artery, you can cut the bullet out. McCall, give me my razor—it's in my saddle wallet."

When McCall handed him the razor, Forsyth opened the shiny blade and offered it to Pliley.

"No, sir!" The frontiersman shook his head stubbornly. "If I cut into that artery, way up there, we couldn't stop the bleeding, never. Your life would be on my hands, Major."

"McCall, you do it!"

The sergeant hesitated only a moment. "Even if it's an order, sir, I can not take the responsibility for putting your life in grave danger."

Forsyth roared: "You're a lot of damned cowards!" And then he laughed gently at the pained astonishment on their faces. "Now, *this* is an order, Sergeant. Put my poncho in your lap, and you others lift me on it." When this was done, Forsyth ordered Pliley to straddle his knee, facing him, while Grover held on tightly to his ankle. "Now, Al, wipe the sand off your hands and press the flesh tight around the bullet." He repressed a cry of pain from the pressure. "Pinch it up so I can get at it!" Forsyth grimly steadied himself, held the razor edge against his aching flesh, and sliced down in one firm motion, prying up the bullet. He lifted it triumphantly. "Don't you see how easy it is now," he cried, and then collapsed in McCall's arms. A burning flood of perspiration flooded into his eyes while Pliley soaked up the blood on his leg with a bandanna handkerchief.

"You were lucky," Pliley said. "You missed the artery."

Forsyth could not summon enough strength to sit erect. McCall slipped a saddlebag beneath his head, and a moment later he was in a deep sleep.

It was late afternoon when he awoke, his shirt soaked with sweat. Most of the ache had gone out of his right thigh, but the shattered bone below his left knee was troubling him now. He wondered if pain had been there all the time, overshadowed by the agony of the bullet's pressure in the other leg. When he rose up to loosen the crude splints, he was surprised to find McCall sitting cross-legged at his feet. The sergeant smiled wearily.

"It's near sundown," Forsyth protested. "You should've waked me before now."

"You've been sleeping like a babe, sir, and it's been a quiet day."

Forsyth scanned both banks of the river. "I see our hostiles are still waiting."

"That's about all they've done all day. Just waiting us out."

A breeze chilled the major's damp shirt, and he pulled his blanket up over his shoulders. "I'm losing track of time, McCall. What day is this?"

"Nineteenth day of September."

"Stilwell and Trudeau have been gone two days." He glanced at the sun setting in a bank of scarlet clouds. "Let me have one of your report blanks. I'm going to send another message to Colonel Bankhead."

With a pencil stub, he began writing:

To Colonel Bankhead, or Commanding Officer, Fort Wallace:

I sent you two messengers on the night of the 17th instant, informing you of my critical situation. If the others have not arrived, then hasten at once to my assistance. I have eight badly wounded and ten slightly wounded men to take in, and every animal I had was killed, save seven, which the Indians stampeded. Lieutenant Beecher is dead, and Acting-Assistant-Surgeon Mooers probably cannot live the night out. He was hit in the head Thursday, and has spoken but one rational word since. I am wounded in two places—in the right thigh and my left leg broken below the knee. The Cheyennes alone number four hundred and fifty or more. Mr. Grover says they never fought so before. They were splendidly armed with Spencer and Henry rifles. We killed at least thirty-five of them, and wounded many more, besides killing and wounding a quantity of their stock. I am on a little island, and have plenty of ammunition left. We are living on mule and horse meat, and are entirely out of rations. If it was not for so many wounded, I would come in, and take the chances of whipping them if attacked. They are evidently sick of the bargain.

I had two of the members of my company killed on the 17th —namely William Wilson and George W. Culver. You had better start with not less than seventy-five men, and bring all the wagons and ambulances you can spare. Bring a six-pound howitzer with you. I can hold out here for six days longer if absolutely necessary, but please lose no time.

> Very respectfully, your obedient servant,
>
> GEORGE A. FORSYTH,
> U.S. Army,
> Commanding Company Scouts.

P.S. —My surgeon having been mortally wounded, none of my wounded have had their wounds dressed yet, so please bring out a surgeon with you.

He folded the paper and glanced up at McCall who was waiting expectantly. "I volunteer," the sergeant said, "to try for Fort Wallace."

"Can't spare you, McCall. Tell Jack Donovan I want to see him. He was mighty eager to go in Trudeau's place the other night."

When Donovan reported he obviously was still eager. "I don't want to brag, Major," he said, "but I wouldn't be surprised if traveling alone I couldn't yet beat Stilwell and French Pete into Fort Wallace."

"You'll not be going alone," Forsyth replied bluntly. "Two men are better than one for such an enterprise. You may choose your companion."

Donovan shrugged. With a finger he flicked sand grains from his long mustache, and then turned his head, looking over the men in their pits as though weighing their relative merits. "All right, sir, I choose Al Pliley. He knows this country."

"A good man," Forsyth agreed. He winked at McCall, adding: "And I don't think he'll endanger you by taking any wild chances."

Before nightfall the cloud banks in the west had overspread the sky, and darkness came down abruptly, a solid wall of blackness. After only a brief ceremony of handshaking, Donovan and Pliley crawled out of the defense circle and vanished silently into the night.

For an hour or so Forsyth sat with McCall, both men listening to sounds in the darkness, occasionally talking softly of their experiences in the Civil War. After the sergeant left to make his rounds of the guards, Forsyth noticed that something had changed. In a second or two he knew what it was. Surgeon Mooers was no longer breathing.

He called for assistance, and several scouts came hurrying through the trench. "He's dead, Major," Grover announced in a solemn voice. They wrapped the surgeon in his blanket, and then carried him out a few yards and covered him with sand.

Forsyth could not fall asleep. He lay thinking of the strangeness of fate, how it tricks all men in different ways. He wondered how fate had treated young Jack Stilwell and old Pete Trudeau, how it would deal with Pliley and Donovan. Suddenly big drops of cold rain struck his face, followed by a steady pelting shower that rattled upon the dried grass. Somewhere above the clouds, southbound geese were honking again. He drew his poncho over his upper body, hoping the rain would make it easier for Al Pliley and Jack Donovan.

18

JOHN DONOVAN

September 20–22

To Donovan it seemed that they were heading west, but Pliley insisted that they were not. "We're pointing straight south," Pliley said.

Some time between midnight and dawn the rain gradually slackened and when the clouds broke apart, Donovan was relieved to find the north star at his back. "Hadn't we ought to turn a little more eastward?" he asked.

"If you want to *walk* all the way to Fort Wallace," Pliley answered patiently. "If we keep going straight south we'll cross the stagecoach trail and maybe ride the rest of the way—if the hostiles haven't stopped the coaches from running."

Donovan said nothing more, but he was glad Pliley was with him; he would never have thought about the stage line, and already his feet were paining him badly. They had both made the mistake of wearing moccasins taken from dead Indians. Rain and mud had softened the leather that was not meant for walking anyway, and every sharp stone and cactus needle was punishment to their feet.

Sunrise caught them on an open plain, but they soon found a mud-caked buffalo wallow with enough high grass around it for concealment as long as they did not stand erect. They took turns sleeping and keeping watch until noon; then they unpacked some of their horsemeat and tried to eat it. To keep from gagging on the spoiled meat, Donovan drank long swallows of water from his canteen until Pliley reminded him that the nearest stream might be twenty miles away.

"Al, you're a smart fellow with lots of common sense," Donovan remarked. "How come you spend your life in this wild Indian country, risking your neck scouting for fifty dollars a month?"

Pliley was sitting cross-legged in his sock feet, scraping dried mud from his trousers. He looked genuinely surprised at Donovan's question, and turned his head to one side like a bird, pondering a reply. "Never gave it much thought, Donovan. I reckon I just plain like this kind of uncomfortable, miserable, foolish way of living."

Donovan laughed. "The boys say you was once thinking on being a doctor."

"Not a word of truth in it," Pliley declared. "When I was mustered out after the war I went in with a lawyer in Topeka to study law. But I couldn't stand being cooped up. First chance I had, I chucked my law books in a corner and headed for Fort Harker to get back with the Army, scouting. I been all over this country round here."

Most of the day the weather was more like spring than autumn, with chill winds that sent black clouds racing across the sky only to be followed by bright sunshine that burned down upon the unshaded buffalo wallow. They saw no animals or human beings until mid-afternoon when Donovan sighted something moving on the western horizon. He awakened Pliley, who confirmed his guess that they were Indians.

"They'll likely turn north," Pliley said. But the Indians kept moving steadily toward the buffalo wallow, and it was soon evident that this was a war party, at least twenty-five warriors, all mounted. "Cheyennes," Pliley declared. "They've seen this rim of grass and may have figured it for a water hole."

"They'll be on us in ten minutes," Donovan said. Both men checked the loads in their carbines and stretched out in prone positions, placing extra cartridges on the ground in easy reach. "You take the left side of their line, I'll take the right. Maybe we'll have time for one reload."

"For a man getting ready to close out his life, you're a cool one, Donovan."

The Cheyennes were no more than three hundred yards away, one of them slightly in the lead. Donovan thought he could see a glint in the Indian's eyes; then suddenly the warrior swung his horse around, halting the others. Across the level prairie, their voices were barely audible. Once during the brief consultation the leader motioned toward the buffalo wallow, and Donovan gripped his carbine tighter.

"Get ready," Pliley whispered.

But the Indians turned away, bearing off in a slow trot to the northeast. Pliley breathed out a long sigh, and said: "He must have told them there was no water here."

Donovan began laughing almost uncontrollably, then started singing. " 'Oh, for a thousand tongues to sing!' Heck, I forget the words of that old song."

"No matter," Pliley said with pretended disgust. "I've heard mules bray better than you sing."

As soon as the sun was down they began moving southward again, walking in long strides, keeping an alert watch along the fading horizon. Donovan was nauseated from the rotten horse-meat, and he could not resist drinking the remainder of his water. He was barely able to keep it down. In a few minutes he was thirsty again. Several times he was certain he could hear a stream running, and would urge Pliley to hurry forward in the darkness, but midnight passed before they reached a river. At the stream's edge, they stripped and waded in, gulping long swallows of the bitter-tasting water, and then bathing their swollen feet.

Pliley decided they were on a fork of Smoky Hill River. "If we take a more westward course," he said, "we should hit the stage road somewhere around Cheyenne Wells. But if the coaches aren't running, we'll have a long track to go by foot."

"How far is it?"

"Maybe fifteen or twenty miles."

"Let's go," Donovan said.

He felt much better after bathing in the river, and for the next hour kept moving steadily. Thick clouds gradually screened out the stars, and in the pitch blackness he occasionally stumbled into beds of prickly pears. Once he had to stop and brush thorns out of his moccasins. "Al, are you sure we're heading in the right direction? I can't see a star or a landmark anywhere."

Pliley pulled up a handful of grass, rolled it in his fingers, smelled and tasted it. "Did you ever notice the grass is different as you go west into Colorado Territory? I think we're going right."

Donovan grunted, and started walking again, dreading the next painful sting of cactus plants which seemed to be lying in wait for him in the darkness. A cold north wind made him shiver, and he felt a few drops of icy rain against his face.

Just before dawn they saw a dim light far ahead, and a few minutes afterward they stumbled into the stagecoach trail. The light was from a lantern hanging in a one-room stage station. As they were passing the corral a herder challenged them. Donovan explained who they were and where they were going. "All we want is a drink of hot coffee, something to eat besides rotten horsemeat, and a place to wait for the eastbound stagecoach."

"That's our business here, mister. Catering to travelers."

"Is the stage still running?" Pliley asked.

"Like a clock," the herder answered proudly. "Eastbound for Fort Wallace due in at six in the morning. I'll go wake up the station master. He does the cooking."

The sleepy station master had hot coffee, saleratus biscuits, and bacon ready for them in an hour, and then they crawled into wall bunks. Donovan was sure he had barely closed his eyes when the herder awoke him with a shout that the stagecoach was arriving.

They rode the fifty miles to Fort Wallace in style, startling their three fellow passengers with accounts of the Indian fight on the Arickaree and the predicament of Major Forsyth and the scouts still trapped there.

Until he stepped off the stage at Fort Wallace, Donovan had

forgotten his swollen, festering feet. He winced as he looked around at the empty parade ground and the deserted barracks. "Where is everybody?"

"Maybe they're at noon mess," Pliley guessed. "It's about that time."

They hobbled across the windy parade to the headquarters building and saw their first soldier—a guard posted beside the entrance steps. He was a thin pale-faced youngster who looked as if he had been dismissed too soon from the hospital. Donovan gave him a mock salute and led the way into the outer office. A gray-haired desk sergeant blinked in surprise.

"We have a message for Colonel Bankhead," Donovan said.

"Lieutenant's in there." The sergeant's voice was unfriendly; he obviously disapproved of their scraggly beards and muddy, grease-stained clothing.

The lieutenant's name was Hugh Johnson. He remained seated when Donovan handed him the folded message. After explaining that Colonel Bankhead was out on patrol, he began reading Forsyth's message. His casual manner quickly changed to alertness. "This is a serious matter. Sergeant!"

The sergeant came in immediately, and in rapid fire order Lieutenant Johnson ordered him to dispatch a telegram to General Sheridan's headquarters, to send a courier out to find Colonel Bankhead, and then to summon every able-bodied male civilian he could find on the post. The gray-haired sergeant said, "Yes, sir," but he went off shaking his head as though the lieutenant had ordered him to perform impossible tasks.

"Sit down." The lieutenant motioned Donovan and Pliley to a bench against the wall. "You boys look tuckered out." His face turned solemn. "We're extremely short of troopers right now. Any good-sized war party could ride right through us. That's why the colonel went out on patrol this morning—he wants to make a show of strength."

"He's got no cause to worry," Pliley said. "Hostiles are all up north, trying to finish off Forsyth's Scouts."

Lieutenant Johnson tapped the desk top with his pencil. "You've had it rough, I know."

Donovan wondered how the lieutenant could know if he hadn't been there. "Stilwell and Trudeau didn't make it through, I guess."

"Who—" The lieutenant glanced at Forsyth's message again. "The two other messengers Major Forsyth sent ahead of you—no, we've seen no trace of them."

A few minutes later the sergeant returned with a telegraph message. As he handed it to the lieutenant, he reported that a courier was on the way to find Bankhead's patrol, and that he had another man out rounding up civilians.

Lieutenant Johnson read the telegram hastily. "Wait a minute. Now I want you to write out a special order, authorizing the quartermaster to pay civilian volunteers a hundred dollars to carry dispatches for the relief of Major Forsyth's Scouts."

"A hundred dollars, sir?" The sergeant's face expressed utter disbelief.

"That's what General Sheridan says. 'Spare no expense of men, money, and horses.' I'll need several good riders who know the country north of here. We haven't much time to reach the cavalry companies up there and start them moving to Forsyth's relief."

"Yes, sir." The sergeant made a note on a piece of paper and went out, closing the door behind him.

Donovan stood up. "I'm one of your volunteers, Lieutenant."

The lieutenant stared at him. "You mean you're willing to start back there right now? In your condition, can you sit a saddle?"

"For a hundred dollars—"

Pliley said: "I can use a hundred, too, Lieutenant. Nothing wrong with us but sore feet. We'll need horses."

"Quartermaster can supply saddle-broken mules, that's all."

"We'll go muleback then."

Outside, a door banged and a husky urgent voice penetrated the thin wall. Pliley's head turned to one side. "Sounds like—"

"Jack Stilwell!" Donovan shouted, and leaped toward the office door, flinging it open.

Stilwell was grinning broadly, but Trudeau looked as if he were ready to collapse. The scouts embraced, danced, slapped each other's backs, and exchanged friendly insults. The lieutenant looked on patiently until Stilwell at last remembered to hand him his message. He reported his meeting with the two Negro couriers en route to Captain Carpenter's camp at Lake Station.

The lieutenant nodded approvingly. "That's the first good news of the day. If the couriers reach him, Captain Carpenter may have his troopers on the way by morning. We'll take no chances, though. I'll start scouts riding north on all military trails within the hour." For the first time since Donovan and Pliley had entered the room, Lieutenant Johnson made a motion to rise. He lifted a pair of crutches from behind the desk, and Donovan was surprised to see that his left leg was swathed in bandages. He put no weight on it as he crossed the office to the outer door.

During the next hour, Donovan was further amazed at how quickly Lieutenant Johnson organized two courier parties. He first sent Al Pliley and another man off toward Frenchman's Fork to search out a company patrolling that area. Then for the ride to Captain Carpenter's cavalry, he put Donovan in command, assigning him three men and eight mules, so they could travel day and night by regular changes of mounts.

Jack Stilwell was eager to go with Donovan, but the lieutenant ordered him to remain at Fort Wallace until Colonel Bankhead returned. "Trudeau is too used up to go anywhere, Stilwell, and the colonel may want you as a guide."

As Donovan and his three scouts mounted their mules to start the long ride, Stilwell was there to shake his hand.

"We've been lucky so far, Donovan," he said. "Let's keep it lucky."

"Sure, Jack." Donovan grinned. "I reckon I kind of low rated you back there on the island."

"Forget it. I'll beat you back there."

Donovan slapped his mule into motion. "Don't bet on it."

Stilwell called after him: "Say, if you see a friend of mine in Captain Carpenter's company, tell him hello. Name's Rube Waller!"

19

trooper
reuben waller

Trooper Reuben Waller was riding as right flanker for Captain Carpenter's 10th Cavalry troop which had been on the march since dawn. They had broken camp near Cheyenne Wells, and were following a long northwesterly bend of the stage road.

Ever since Waller had delivered Jack Stilwell's message and map to Captain Carpenter, the captain seemed to be in a fretful, impatient mood. That morning he had roused his men out of their blankets in chilly darkness, cut the breakfast hour in half, and had been pushing the column so hard all morning that horses and men were beginning to show signs of exhaustion. Waller was hopeful that any minute now the captain would call a long halt for nooning.

Every two or three minutes, Waller turned in his saddle and slowly scanned the eastern horizon from north to south. The sky was cloudy but the air was clear except where strong gusts of wind kicked up little swirls of dust here and there. He studied each dust swirl carefully until it disappeared; then he pulled his horse into line with the column again.

Reuben Waller was proud to be a member of the 10th Cavalry, especially Troop H which Captain Carpenter called "the cock of the roost." Sometimes Waller found it hard to believe all the things that had happened to him in six years. He marked the beginning of his new life with the day he rode off with his master from the big Mississippi plantation house. He was a slave then and was going to help his master fight the Yankees. He remembered he had been scared and excited, but after the first battle he grew accustomed to the noise and confusion. He reckoned he must have survived twenty-nine battles in all; then his master was captured somewhere in Virginia.

After that Reuben Waller wandered around until one day he heard the war was ended, and it seemed as if just about everybody white and black was heading west to make their fortunes. By hiring out to drive wagon teams, he reached Fort Leavenworth, and when he heard that a captain named Carpenter was recruiting Negroes for cavalry service he decided to apply. "I was not a regular soldier, understand, sir," he told Captain Carpenter, "but I rode with the Confederate cavalry through twenty-nine battles."

Captain Carpenter had laughed and asked him if he rode with Forrest or Jackson.

"With both generals, sir," Waller replied truthfully.

"Then we were probably shooting at each other in the Shenandoah," Carpenter declared, and signed him up as a private in the U.S. 10th Cavalry.

A little more than a year ago, Waller remembered, he had started soldiering in a blue uniform. Now he glanced again with pride at the weary but cleanly aligned column moving on his left—seventy men with black faces, and a scattering of white civilian scouts. The thirteen wagons and single ambulance in the rear were beginning to kick up considerable dust.

The dust reminded him to scan the eastern horizon again, and this time there was something different about it, a tiny concentration of movement that was more than a sand swirl. For a minute or two he stared at the blur of motion until he was certain it was several horsemen riding fast. Then he placed two fingers between his teeth, shrilling a whistle, and when he saw that he had attracted the attention of Lieutenant Orleman, he swung his wide-brimmed hat above his head and pointed eastward. The lieutenant immediately spurred his horse forward to join Captain Carpenter, and a few moments later the captain signaled Waller to come in.

When Waller rode up beside him, the captain was still watching the oncoming riders through his field glass. "Not Indians," he said, "but they're not soldiers, either." He handed Waller the field glass. "See if they're the two scouts who gave you Major Forsyth's map."

Waller focused the glass, trying to recognize the faces through the dust. There were four men on four mules and leading four, but he was soon satisfied that neither Jack Stilwell not the old Frenchman, Trudeau, was with them. "No, sir," he replied. "But I think I've seen one of them before, a muleskinner from the quartermaster's at Fort Wallace."

Captain Carpenter breathed out a long sigh. He was a heavy-set man with a wide flowing brown mustache bleached by the sun. He took the glass back and for another minute held it on the riders. Then he turned to Lieutenant Orleman. "I hope Colonel Bankhead's not ordering us back there. We're Major Forsyth's only hope." He sighed again. "All right, Private Waller, ride out and escort them in."

Waller moved away at a trot, gradually increasing pace to an easy gallop. In a few minutes he was in hailing distance, and he heard the lead rider calling: "Captain Carpenter's 10th Cavalry?" Waller shouted back that it was Carpenter's cavalry, and slowed his tired mount, letting the mules close the distance.

"I'm Jack Donovan," the lead rider said, "with a message for Captain Carpenter."

Waller nodded politely and wheeled his horse, leading them in at a brisk trot. On the way in, Donovan asked him if the captain had received the verbal message sent by Jack Stilwell. Waller showed his teeth in a big grin, and replied that he had been the messenger.

"Then why is the captain still marching on the stage road? He ought to be bearing more to the north."

"You'd better ask the captain that question, Mr. Donovan,"

Waller replied good-naturedly. "Captain Carpenter don't confide his plans with privates like me."

A few minutes later, Donovan was asking Captain Carpenter the question, and Carpenter replied gruffly that the map sent by Stilwell was rather sketchy, and that because of his wagons he wanted to stay on a well-beaten trail as long as possible before cutting across rough country. "See here, Donovan, or whatever your name is, I'm just as anxious as you are to get to Major Forsyth's position. He and I served together in the Shenandoah."

Donovan finished wiping dust off his beard with a bandanna; then he casually presented the message written by Lieutenant Johnson at Fort Wallace. Carpenter unfolded the paper, fumbled in his blouse pockets for a minute, finally cried out in exasperation as he passed the message to Lieutenant Orleman. "Confound it, Lieutenant, I must have stowed my reading spectacles in my pack. Read it to me."

Lieutenant Orleman began reading in a loud parade-ground voice, his accent slightly German:

The commanding officer directs you to proceed at once to a point on the Dry Fork of the Republican, about seventy-five or eighty miles north, northwest from this point, thirty or forty miles west by a little south from the forks of the Republican, with all possible despatch.

Two scouts from Major Forsyth's command arrived here this evening and bring word that he (Forsyth) was attacked on the morning of Thursday last by an overpowering force of Indians (seven hundred) who killed all the animals, broke Major Forsyth's leg with a rifle ball and severely wounded him in the groin, wounded Surgeon Mooers in the head and wounded Lieutenant Beecher in several places. Two men of the command were killed and eighteen or twenty wounded.

HUGH JOHNSON
First Lieutenant, 5th Infantry,
Acting Post Adjutant.

When the lieutenant finished, Captain Carpenter was gazing northward across the dry plain. He sniffed, and turned to Donovan. "It's worse even than I thought. Can you lead us back there by tomorrow night?"

"I can try," Donovan replied. "With your wagons it might take another day."

"To save Major Forsyth I must take the risk of dividing my troop," Carpenter said gravely. He glanced at Waller, who had pulled his horse off to one side awaiting further orders.

"Trooper Waller, ride back down the column and ask Dr. Fitzgerald and all civilian scouts to report up here to me. And Lieutenant Orleman, you will order the men to dismount and loosen saddles. We'll halt for twenty minutes to eat and rest."

In less than five minutes, Waller returned with Dr. Fitzgerald and the scouts. Everyone was dismounted now, the troopers reclining, some of them beginning to chew their cold rations. The scouts, the surgeon, and two lieutenants gathered around Captain Carpenter. Waller sat cross-legged nearby, listening to them plan a fast march to relieve Major Forsyth.

"Food and medicine are Forsyth's desperate needs," the captain was saying. "Donovan assures me the men are well fortified on their island and have enough ammunition to keep the hostiles at bay for several days. But rations are exhausted, the surgeon is unconscious, perhaps already dead, and there is no medicine for the festering wounds of some twenty men. To get enough food and medicine there will require at least one vehicle. I propose using the ambulance which is much faster than a wagon. To get the ambulance and Dr. Fitzgerald through the besieging Indians will require a heavily armed escort. Now, there are seventeen of you scouts. Eight of you enlisted at Sheridan's headquarters for service with Forsyth's Scouts but arrived too late at Fort Wallace to join the expedition. The other nine were enlisted for miscellaneous duties out of Wallace. I'm asking all of you to volunteer for this extra-hazardous duty."

Without exception the scouts volunteered, their voices mingling at the end in a resounding shout.

Donovan raised his hand. "My three men and I will go along with them, of course."

"I was counting on you to guide them, Mr. Donovan," the captain replied dryly. "Now, Lieutenant Orleman, you will select thirty good troopers from both platoons. Look for the soundest horses and the best shots. I'd like the scouts to lead off with Donovan as guide, followed by the ambulance and Dr. Fitzgerald, with Lieutenant Orleman and his platoon closing the rear. Meanwhile, Lieutenant Banzhaf will bring on the wagons—the men on that island will need the supplies they carry. Lieutenant Banzhaf, I want those wagons kept rolling. If some mules begin to fail, you may cut loose two or three wagons and abandon them, rather than slow to the pace of the weakest animals. Naturally the rear is going to fall far behind the first section, perhaps several miles, and I'm going to need a courier to keep me informed as to where the wagons are and if they are in any danger. Trooper Waller! Where are you?"

Waller came forward and the captain said brusquely: "Trooper Waller, stand by for special courier duty. Now, you civilian gentlemen, as soon as you've swallowed your rations and taken a sip of water, prepare to move out. Lieutenant Orleman, you may start assembling your platoon. Dr. Fitzgerald and I will go back and personally supervise the loading of the ambulance with hardtack, coffee, and bacon."

A few minutes later, Jack Donovan rode out with the scouts, turning off the stage road and heading straight northward. Three hundred yards behind them rolled the ambulance, careening from side to side as its narrow wheels bounced over tufts of bunch grass. In its rear, just out of reach of the dust, rode Captain Carpenter and Lieutenant Orleman, followed by thirty selected men of H Troop. The column's gait was an alternate walk and trot that with the passing of every hour brought them closer to Major Forsyth's besieged scouts.

For the first hour, Trooper Waller rode a few yards to the right of the guidon; then at a signal from Captain Carpenter he dropped back to the rear. His instructions were to keep Lieutenant Banzhaf's wagon train in view as long as possible. When it was no longer visible, he was to begin riding back and forth between the two sections, changing mounts when necessary, always keeping a close watch along the rim of the entire horizon, and reporting to the lieutenant or the captain anything out of the ordinary.

Trooper Waller was thinking again about how lucky he was to be horse-soldiering with Troop H. He was proud of his assignment and pleased that Captain Carpenter believed in him. Sometimes the captain was as rough as a cob, but he was for certain one white soldier a black soldier could put his trust in—that Captain Louis Carpenter.

20

captain
Louis carpenter

September 23–25

Until sundown Captain Carpenter kept the first section of his column moving in its monotonous rhythm of walks and trots, broken hourly by short halts. He would have marched on for another hour had not one of the scouts reported back that a pair of water holes just ahead offered the last camping site for several miles.

As the wagon train was only four or five miles in the rear, he sent Trooper Waller back with orders to Lieutenant Banzhaf to bring the wagons on in the darkness. By nine o'clock the two sections were rejoined, the wagons corraled, horses and mules picketed, guards out. Every man free of duties was grateful for a chance to roll up in his blanket for a short night of rest and sleep.

Before dawn Carpenter was up, waking the bugler and ordering cooking fires started. At daylight the scouts moved out, followed by the ambulance and the first section of troopers.

In less than half an hour, Jack Donovan came galloping back to report fresh Indian sign. Motioning to the first set of fours to join them as an escort, Carpenter hurried forward with Donovan. Half a mile ahead, they found the other scouts still poking around a hastily abandoned Indian camp.

"They vamoosed in a hurry," Donovan said, pointing to three saddles that had been left by a willow clump. They were pad saddles, fully equipped with stirrups and girths, and Carpenter knew that only badly frightened Indians would have left them behind.

"My guess is there were more squaws than warriors in this camp," Carpenter said. "Survivors of the fight with Major Forsyth, perhaps. Probably heard our bugle this morning and thought we were charging down on them. What do you think, Donovan?"

"Makes sense. But if they've quit the battlefield, what's happened to Forsyth's Scouts?"

Carpenter shook his head. "If we're going to find out today," he replied, "we'd better get moving. Lead your men out."

He waited with his escort until Lieutenant Orleman arrived with the ambulance. His first order was to the bugler; there would be no more bugle calls until further notice.

Late in the evening Carpenter sighted a line of willows and small cottonwoods, and when he raised his field glass he saw the scouts halted there, evidently waiting for him. With his escort he hurried forward. As he had guessed, the willows edged a stream bed, but there was not even a trickle running, only a few water holes fed by seepage under the sands.

Donovan looked confident. "This must be the Dry Fork, or the Arickaree as Sharp Grover calls it," he said. "Our island should be about fifteen or twenty miles upstream."

Carpenter called a short noon halt to let the horses drink from the water holes. He then sent Trooper Waller back to Lieutenant Banzhaf with instructions to turn the wagon train northwestward, keeping the Dry Fork on his right, but remaining some distance from it because of gullies and ridges near the watercourse.

For the next fifteen miles Carpenter rode with Donovan. Whenever they approached a ridge or small rise, both men pushed their horses forward eagerly, hoping to see some sign that would assure them they were nearing the island. "It just don't look right to me, Captain," Donovan finally admitted. "The stream's narrowing too

fast. That island's north, not west the way we're going. I'm sure of
it."

Carpenter unfolded the worn map that Forsyth had given Jack
Stilwell; with restrained impatience he examined it for the hun-
dredth time. "This map shows only one fork running into the Republican River."

"I'll wager a month's pay there's two, maybe three forks," Donovan insisted.

Carpenter squinted at the sun, hating it for being so low in the
sky. "I wanted to find Forsyth before dark." He turned in his
saddle and beckoned hastily to the troopers to close up on the
guidon. They had become strung out because of the ambulance
which had to detour around some of the deeper washes. "We'll ride
to that next ridge and then bear north," he said, and urged his
horse forward again.

At the first easy crossing beyond the ridge, they left the Dry
Fork and faced northward. An hour before sunset they struck a
downslope and in a few minutes were in thick grass, with another
willow-fringed valley before them.

"Indian trail," Donovan cried. "Over to the right!"

When Carpenter reined up beside the scout, he was surprised at
the breadth of the trail. The other men gathered around, dismounted, carefully examined the markings, and then began offering various opinions as to the size of the party. "At least two
thousand ponies," Donovan declared. "And plenty of travois
scratches. A whole village. They came down the valley to graze
their ponies here and then headed north."

"This must be the Arickaree Fork." Carpenter's voice was
harsh. For the second time that day he was depressed by his failure
to defeat time and distance. *If the Indians were leaving,* he wondered, *what had happened to Forsyth's Scouts?*

"How old is the trail?" he asked.

"Only a few hours," Donovan replied, and one of the other
scouts volunteered an opinion that the Indians had crossed no
earlier than noon.

"Let's move on to the river and have a look at it," Carpenter
said, and put his horse into a slow walk. *Two thousand ponies,* he

thought, *means a thousand or at least several hundred warriors. They could take my thirty troopers quicker than they did Forsyth's fifty scouts.* He shook off his apprehension and studied the lay of the land.

Less than a mile to the west was a hill that could be easily defended. Or if the wagons could be brought up and corraled, they could camp by the river which had a good flow of water in it. He glanced at the sun, was dismayed at how close it was to the horizon, and then made a quick decision. "Lieutenant Orleman, take half your platoon and ride back to the train. Tell Banzhaf you're bringing the wagons in here before dark if you have to lash the mules all the way."

Orleman looked surprised, but wasted no time in choosing his men; they wheeled and started back at a fast trot.

Carpenter dismounted, removed his boots and socks, and waded into the stream. He joined Surgeon Fitzgerald on a sand bar, and the two men sat cooling their feet until the sun was level with the horizon. He called Donovan then, and ordered him to mount up the scouts. "We're going to cross over and climb that hill." He turned to a sergeant who was resting by the ambulance. "Sergeant, station your men in defensive positions. We'll be back before dark."

The hill was not as steep as it had seemed from the river, and in a few minutes Carpenter, the surgeon, and the scouts were almost to the summit. Under cover of the last ridge-fold they halted, left their mounts with two horseholders, and began climbing on foot. Just before reaching the top Carpenter bent low, peering over the crest. He sucked in his breath. For a second he thought he was looking upon a battlefield. Below him was a lesser hill, its eastward slope dotted with dead horses and burial scaffolds.

"Dead Indians," Dr. Fitzgerald said. "They lost more than a few."

With his field glass, Carpenter carefully studied the panorama before him, following the freshly beaten trail of the Indians until it faded into blue twilight, tracing the winding river hopefully for the besieged island. Nothing moved anywhere; no fires glimmered; there was no sound but the whisper of a rising wind against tall grass.

After summoning the horseholders to bring up the mounts, Carpenter posted guards on the hilltop, and rode across to the burial slope. Each blanketed body lay on a pole scaffold, feet pointed to the east. Beside each scaffold were one or more slain horses that had belonged to the warriors.

"What a waste of horseflesh," Carpenter said.

"They believe a dead warrior needs a horse to ride to the happy hunting grounds," Fitzgerald replied. "Who knows?"

Most of the scaffolds appeared to be three or four days old. To make certain that the dead had been killed in battle, Carpenter ordered one of the bodies brought down from its eight-foot platform. The warrior had died from carbine fire.

"Put the body back in its proper position," Carpenter said. He heard Donovan calling his name from farther up the slope. "Over here, Captain!"

Donovan had his rifle cocked, was pointing it into a shallow ravine. Not twenty yards away stood a lone tepee of freshly tanned buffalo skins.

"What is it?" Carpenter asked.

"I don't know. That tepee's never been used. No soot around the smoke hole."

"Let's have a look."

"I'll cover you," Donovan said.

Pistol in hand, Carpenter approached the silent tepee. Lifting the closed flap slowly, he peered inside. He holstered his pistol and entered. In the dim light he could see the form of a warrior wrapped in a white buffalo robe and lying on a low brush framework surrounded by weapons and a flowing warbonnet.

Carpenter lifted the buffalo robe; the Indian's face still bore its warpaint. *He has a stern and royal look,* Carpenter thought, and then heard Donovan behind him. "Roman Nose?" Carpenter asked.

"Yeah." Donovan's voice was solemn. "That's Roman Nose."

Just as darkness fell the wagons arrived and crossed the river. Carpenter corraled them in a tight circle, doubled guards, and ordered the off-duty men to sleep with rifles at ready. He had trouble falling asleep. For most of the night, a cold fitful wind

howled eerily, and when he did sleep he dreamed that he had
found the island but all the scouts were dead, scalped, and brutally
mutilated. He got up in the darkness, listening to the wind and the
gentle murmur of the river, debating whether he should disturb his
men so early. *This is the morning of September 25,* he thought. *Can
Forsyth's Scouts have endured to this ninth day of siege, without
food, medicine, or reinforcements?* He shook Lieutenant Orleman
awake and told him to prepare the column for marching before
daylight.

Although there was barely any light in the sky when the scouts
rode out, they had little trouble backtracking the broad trail left by
the Indians. At sunup they were on the crest of a ridge, and Carpenter could follow the river's sandy channel through his field
glass. For several miles the stream made a wide bend, and the trail
split into divergent tracks that cut across rolling country gashed by
deep gullies.

"Donovan," he called softly. "Have a look through this glass—
at the farther bend of the stream."

After looking for a few moments, Donovan shook his head. "I'm
not quite sure, Captain, but I think the island's a little farther up
the river." He shifted the glass slightly. "Wait a minute! Yes, by
. . . There's the island!" He pointed excitedly. "I can see some of
the scouts. They're still alive!"

Carpenter whirled and shouted to Lieutenant Orleman: "Take
half of your platoon, Lieutenant, and escort the ambulance around
by the river valley trail. I'll take the others with the scouts and
make a dash across the breaks. Let's move out!"

He led the way down the steep slope, hooves thundering behind
him, and urged his mount impatiently over the next ridge. After
crossing a series of thicketed gullies, they drove hard up the last
rise before the river. Here Carpenter signaled a halt so that he
could scan the open country for hostiles.

Not an Indian was in sight. The tiny island seemed deserted.
Overhead in the cloudy sky, buzzards were circling. A drift of
wind told him why; the air was heavy with the stench of rotting
flesh.

As he was turning to ask Donovan if he was certain he had seen any of Forsyth's Scouts, his eyes caught a movement just below. A man had scurried out of a plum thicket and was running toward the island. Carpenter shouted at him, started his horse forward, and the others came on behind him at a fast trot.

Suddenly the man stopped, turned, and raised his carbine to take aim.

"Spread out! Wave your hats!" Carpenter commanded, and then bellowed at the man: "Don't shoot! We're friends!"

For a second the man remained frozen; then he tossed his carbine in the air and began cheering. Beyond him on the island, Carpenter saw other scouts crawling from their sand pits. Some were shouting, some running, some hobbling unsteadily. They looked like gaunt wolves.

Carpenter wondered if he had arrived too late to save his old friend, Sandy Forsyth.

21

MAJOR GEORGE
(SANDY) FORSYTH

September 25

On the morning of the ninth day of the siege, Major Forsyth lay on his canvas stretcher watching the sun rise. He knew that he was feverish and that for some days dreams and reality had blended so that he was never certain whether he was asleep or awake.

By mustering all his strength he was able to turn himself and count the row of twigs he had pressed into the side of the sand pit. There were eight. With his right hand he searched in the sand until he found another twig and added it to the row. As he closed his eyes he thought: One more day to endure.

"I brought you some soup, Major."

He opened his eyes again and recognized Chance Whitney. The putrid odor of the soup nauseated him. "Don't we have any more of that coyote that Slinger shot last night?" He was surprised at the irritable tone in his own voice.

"Schlesinger shot that coyote three days ago, Major," the scout replied patiently. Whitney had large droopy eyelids that gave him a perpetually sad expression. "We boiled that coyote's head and bones over and over till there was no shred of nutriment left. Here, take some of this watery plum jelly."

Forsyth managed to raise himself long enough to swallow the cooked plums. "Nothing left now but plums and prickly pears," he said, and looked directly into Whitney's mournful eyes. "If no relief comes today, Chance, I shall order all you able-bodied scouts to try to make your escape."

Whitney shook his head. "You've had our answer to that proposition already, Major. Some of the boys are looking for prairie dogs this morning. We'll make it."

"No one should have left the island without my permission." Forsyth's voice was querulous.

"Mr. Grover sent them, sir. He says the Indians have gone off."

Again Forsyth tried to raise his body on the canvas. "All of them?" He shaded his eyes to peer at the low bluffs across the Arickaree. "Even the vedette they've had observing us the past two days?"

"Not an Indian in sight anywhere this morning," Whitney assured him.

Forsyth sagged back on the canvas, too weak to talk any more. He was thinking that after a while he must order the able-bodied men to try to save themselves, and then he remembered how loyally obstinant they had been—when was it, two or three days ago? —whenever it was that he gave them permission to escape.

He had warned them that the four scouts sent to Fort Wallace might have failed to get through, and that possibly no relief party would ever come. Then he had said that those who were able to go were at liberty to make a try to save themselves.

Sergeant McCall had asked: "Who will take care of the wounded?"

"Those of us who are unable to go must take our chances," Forsyth replied.

For a moment there was a dead silence, then McCall shouted: "Never! We'll stand by to the end, if it must be." Martin Burke had added quickly: "Walk away and leave our wounded to them red devils! No, sir! We've fought together, and by heaven, if needs be we'll die together." As each scout refused one by one to leave,

Burke picked up a long stick, tied his blue sailor jacket to it, and
thrust it upright into the sand. Hands on hips, he stood back and
admired it. "There," he cried. "That's our flag of no surrender!"

The scouts were held together by something stronger than mere
military discipline, Forsyth thought . . . but it all seemed so long
ago . . . there was dried horsemeat then but now there was nothing but the stench of rotting animals . . . the Indians were gone
. . . he must order the men who were able to walk to make a try
at saving themselves . . . some of them were beginning to turn
crazy, sometimes refusing to talk and sometimes talking like luna-
tics.

He could hear Burke talking now, in the adjoining sand pit.
"Wake up, Oakes, the Indians are gone. You'd better walk around
a bit to keep your arrow wound open so it'll heal from the inside. If
it closes up outside you'll have a bad time, for certain."

George Oakes grumbled profanely about being waked out of the
only pleasant dream he'd had on the island. "I was dreaming I had
this nice piece of buffalo hump and was just opening my watering
mouth to chew down on it when you had to go and wake me up,
Burke."

"Look over there!" The Irishman's voice was suddenly filled
with excitement. "Must be somebody coming."

"More Indians," Oakes said disgustedly.

From across the defense circle a scout shouted: "Indians coming
back!"

Forsyth pulled himself upright. Several men were out of their
pits, staring toward the low line of hills beyond the grass flats.
"Some of our boys are out there hunting for game!" another scout
cried. "We'd better organize a rescue party."

"Hold on a minute!" The voice was Sharp Grover's. He dropped
into Forsyth's pit, and picked up the major's field glass. "There are
some moving objects on the far hills, Major." After a moment he
dropped the glass back on the canvas. His usually tight lips were
relaxed in a faint smile.

"Are they Indians?" Oakes shouted.

"They don't ride like Indians," Grover answered. "Boys, there
comes our relief!"

"Are you certain?" Forsyth asked.

"They're wearing blue, Major, and coming in fast."

The scouts were already swinging their hats and cheering. Like a whirling jumping-jack, Schlesinger circled the pits in a lunatic's dance, laughing until tears came into his eyes. Dick Gantt, although badly wounded, was using his carbine as a crutch and jigging on one leg; he joined hands with Schlesinger and almost fell, laughing wildly.

With his field glass Forsyth found the lead horseman. "By all the wonders," he said. "It's Louis Carpenter and his Brunettes!" Morning sunshine glittered on the cavalrymen's sabers and carbines; wind whipped their single guidon.

"They're buffalo soldiers, all right," Grover agreed. "I can see their white teeth grinning at us from their black faces. And, Major, if you'll take a look down the valley you'll see more of them, bringing in an ambulance."

"Glory be!" Forsyth's voice broke under the strain. "Carpenter thought of everything. An ambulance means that a surgeon must be with them."

"I'll mosey down and meet him," Grover said. "No one on this island needs a doc more than you do, Major."

Forsyth was having trouble keeping moisture out of his eyes. He watched Carpenter coming on in that familiar easy lope he'd favored when they were riding together in the Shenandoah. They'd always been friendly rivals, trying to outdo each other in imperturbability, composure under stress. Carpenter always called it *sangfroid*. Well, he'd show Carpenter some *sangfroid* now. He reached under the canvas stretcher, found his dog-eared copy of Dickens' *Oliver Twist,* turned his back to the approaching cavalrymen and pretended to be reading.

He could hear the hoofbeats on the sand. Most of the riders halted outside the defense circle but one came on slowly to Forsyth's pit. The tired horse snuffled, saddle leather creaked, boots scrunched against sand. Forsyth carefully folded the corner of a page in his book, closed it, turned slowly and looked up at Louis Carpenter. "Captain Carpenter," he said, "you're late in reporting."

Carpenter opened his mouth, started to laugh, but could not conceal his concern over Forsyth's weakened appearance. "Don't try to pull rank on me, Sandy Forsyth," he growled. He rubbed a forefinger across his bleached mustache, frowning at the devastated island, and then jerked a bandanna from his pocket and buried his nose in it against the stench of decaying animals. "You keep a mighty malodorous camp, Major Forsyth. Would never pass inspection." He knelt beside the canvas stretcher, removed a gauntlet, and offered his hand. "How are you, you old rawhider?"

A few minutes later the ambulance rolled onto the island, and Grover and the surgeon joined them. "This is Dr. Jenkins Fitzgerald, Major Forsyth," Carpenter said. "He'll soon have you back in a saddle."

Forsyth showed Dr. Fitzgerald where his two wounds were, and while the surgeon unwrapped the dirty bandages for closer examination, he tried to keep his mind off the pain by watching the scouts' noisy reception of the troopers.

In front of his pit, Negro cavalrymen were emptying their haversacks of rations, distributing them among the scouts. One huge trooper lent his arm to crippled Dick Gantt who was saying: "When you boys rode over that slope, it was the prettiest sight I ever did see."

The Negro smiled and looked closely at Gantt. "From your talk, I reckon you must be a Southern boy?"

"Mississippi," Gantt replied.

"Me, too. What you doing here with all these Yankees?"

Gantt stopped chewing on his mouthful of bacon. "You know, I been asking myself that question for the last nine days."

Dr. Fitzgerald stood up to ease the strain on his back. He glanced at the group of scouts and troopers. "Captain Carpenter," he said, "if you don't want a pack of sick scouts on your hands and mine, you'd better order your troopers to stop stuffing them. Nothing will give a starving man stomach cramps quicker than hardtack and raw bacon."

Carpenter immediately shouted an order to a sergeant to stop his men from distributing food.

"Another thing we must do right now," the surgeon continued, "is move off this reeking island."

Forsyth suggested that the high ground to the east would be the best vantage point for a new camp, and in a few minutes the transfer was under way. Using stretchers from the ambulance, troopers carried the sick and wounded across the riverbed and then for a quarter of a mile up the slope. Before the task was completed, Lieutenant Banzhaf's wagon train arrived, tents were unloaded, and a makeshift field hospital hastily established. Under the busy surgeon's direction a detail of troopers also began preparing hot bacon soup and coffee for the famished scouts.

After swallowing some of the soup, Forsyth fell asleep under an open tent shelter, and it was late afternoon when he awoke again to find Dr. Fitzgerald sitting on a camp stool beside him. "Major," the surgeon said, "I'm going to be direct with you. Your fever is worse, indicating what I suspected when I examined you this morning. Your shattered leg is filled with poison."

"Yes?"

"I must advise amputation."

Forsyth gripped the edges of his cot with his hands. "Suppose I say no?"

"I can't force you to a decision. Amputation is dangerous in a hospital, doubly dangerous out here, but the poison is spreading."

"What are my chances if I say no?"

Fitzgerald shrugged. "Perhaps fifty-fifty. But if your condition worsens for another twenty-four hours, undoubtedly it will be too late to amputate."

For several seconds Forsyth stared at his bandaged leg; then he said firmly: "I refuse permission to amputate."

Fitzgerald sighed. "Then I must drain your leg, set your shattered bones, and try to clean out the poisoned lacerations with carbolic acid. The pain will be excruciating. You must be given chloroform of course."

Hours later Forsyth was dreaming that he was in a deep cave. He was struggling to reach the entrance which seemed to be whirling and growing narrower. Calm voices sounded from nearby, and only by the greatest effort of will was he able to raise his eyelids.

"You're doing splendidly, Major," Fitzgerald said. He lifted Forsyth's shoulders while a trooper placed a folded blanket beneath so that he could sit partially erect. "You may feel nauseous after a few minutes," the surgeon continued. "If so, just let go."

As his vision cleared, Forsyth was surprised at the enormity of his left leg. "You must have used barrel staves for splits," he said.

"Used the trunk of a cottonwood tree," Fitzgerald replied. "Halved it, hollowed it, and packed it with cotton. After all the labor I spent putting your shattered shinbone back together, I don't mean for it to be shaken loose on the way back to Fort Wallace."

Forsyth noticed a small detail of men at work on the slope below. He had seen enough such details to know what they were doing; they were burying the dead. A trooper was driving stakes into the ground at the head of each grave. Just behind the trooper, Sergeant McCall was hammering an empty cartridge into each stake. In his thorough way, McCall had written the name of each dead scout on a piece of paper and rolled it into an empty cartridge for later identification.

"Beecher, Mooers, Culver, Wilson," Forsyth said softly. "But I count five graves. Who was the fifth man?"

"Farley. The older one, Lewis Farley. If we could have arrived a day or two earlier I might have saved him, but his arm was gangrenous, too near the heart. His boy takes it hard."

"Yes, I remember. Farley lost his wife in an Indian raid." Forsyth gazed at a graying bank of clouds in the west. The sun was already down. "How are the other wounded scouts?"

"They're tough as oaks; they'll make it." Fitzgerald turned at the sound of approaching footsteps. In the first dull light of dusk, Forsyth recognized the sturdy silhouette of Louis Carpenter striding up the slope. He was carrying a pair of boots slung over his shoulder.

Carpenter's voice rasped at the surgeon: "How is he?"

"He'll do," Fitzgerald replied.

Another and much thinner silhouette appeared behind Carpenter. "The scouts want to know how the major is." It was Schlesinger's voice.

"Tell them I still have my leg in spite of the surgeon," Forsyth said.

"Can I bring you anything, sir?"

"Not a thing, Slinger, thank you."

Carpenter dropped the boots he was carrying beside Forsyth's cot. "Sergeant McCall said you should have them. They were Lieutenant Beecher's."

"Fred Beecher. The finest young officer I ever knew." Forsyth blinked at the darkening sky. "Beecher never liked boots. Preferred Indian moccasins." He turned his head and was surprised to see Schlesinger still standing there, watching anxiously. The boy's cheap shoes were cracked and broken. "Slinger, take these boots. Lieutenant Beecher would want you to have them."

"Thank you, sir. It's an honor."

"If they fit, wear them."

"Yes, sir."

Forsyth closed his eyes, fighting nausea. He could smell smoke from the evening's first cooking fires, scented with cedar. Faintly, then more strongly came the sound of singing voices, the troopers singing a mournful song. He remembered Virginia, the cedar smoke of campfires in the Shenandoah, and resonant Negro voices singing sadly out of the darkness.

Fitzgerald's hand touched his forehead. "Your fever is down," the surgeon said.

"They don't make them any flintier than Major Forsyth," Carpenter declared. "By the way, Sandy," he added, "I've started writing my report, but I don't know how to head it. What do they call this place, that island down there?"

Forsyth stared hard at the captain. "I don't know how the Indians or the map makers name it," he said slowly. "But forever in my memory it will be Beecher's Island."

Wresting the weapon from her, I pushed her back against the moss. "Stay down," I said. She was breathing hard from fright and excitement, her bright blue eyes burning with hatred. "Medicine Woman was right," she said after a minute. "We should have killed you. Now you have brought the bluecoats to kill us."

I watched the platoon moving in fast along the creek. "I had no choice," I said. "But if Red Eagle will surrender, there won't be any squaw-killing."

She sucked in her breath and hissed her opinion of me through her bared teeth. "The Cheyenne will never surrender to become prisoners. Medicine Woman has gone to tell Red Eagle the white man's soldiers have come again. The Cheyenne will send many bluecoats to the land of ghosts before they can kill us all."

I turned around and peered through the brush, following the progress of the platoon. The lieutenant in command had slowed his men to a walk. His head jerked back and forth as he watched nervously. He didn't like the look of the silent bluff. At the edge of the creek, facing the bluff, he halted the platoon and sent a messenger back to Captain Anderson.

I turned to the girl: "Where is Dunreath—my friend, the old man?"

"He will die with much suffering," she said bitterly, her face turned away from me.

"Where is he?"

"In the woods near Red Eagle's lodge. The Dog Soldiers will know what to do with that one."

Firing sounded from somewhere beyond the bluff, a few desultory reports. I guessed that D Troop had run into Cheyenne pickets somewhere on the other side. Marisa raised herself, standing close beside me in the dugout, looking back toward the bluff.

Evidently Captain Anderson had also heard the firing. He ordered all of B Troop into a gallop, and the horsemen raced forward to join the advance platoon. Anderson's voice echoed back; he was dismounting the first platoon, starting the men on foot across the iced-over creek.

Before they reached the bottom of the bluff, a line of blanketed squaws appeared on the rim above them. I could see smoke from their muzzle-loaders before I heard the sounds of firing. Two of the dismounted soldiers went down; the others hugged the footing of the bluff.

While some of the squaws were reloading, others ran forward and began dropping rocks, logs, frozen dirt—anything they could lay hands on—down upon the men below.

As the dismounted platoon began breaking ranks in retreat across the ice, a bugle blasted recall. I whirled around in the dugout. Out on the front, Colonel Comstock was calling B Troop back, and was sending the twelve-pounder Napoleon gun forward. He didn't want a close-in fight.

Captain Anderson retrieved his two casualties and pulled B Troop back in an orderly withdrawal, reassembling them directly behind the twelve-pounder. Some of the batterymen were swinging picks into the icy ground, others were digging with shovels. Within a few minutes they had dug a narrow pit and were sinking the trail of the gun deep to gain a high elevation. I remembered that trick from Vicksburg. By using a small charge of powder, the gunners could obtain a dropping mortar fire upon the Cheyennes on the bluff.

Marisa was crying softly. *At least she's safe, out of range,* I thought. "You're my prisoner, Marisa," I said gently. "We'll ride back to the soldiers' pack mules. You'll be safe there."

She squirmed down into the moss at the dugout's bottom and began pounding her fists against my boots. From across the snow field came the gunnery sergeant's commands; there was a moment of quiet, and then the screaming swish of the missile, the roar of the gun, the hollow echoes of explosion. They had overshot, and there was some delay while the forward observer signaled back and adjustments were made. The second shell exploded directly in center atop the bluff. Snow, earth, and rocks flew up in a dark cloud, followed by a high eerie screaming.

A moment later I was startled to see a Cheyenne riding forward around the bend of the creek. The rider was Red Eagle in his warbonnet, carrying a white rag on a ramrod. He was not hurrying his horse; it was as if he were riding aimlessly with all the time in the world. I glanced back at the twelve-pounder, expecting to see its batterymen standing in waiting positions. Instead, they were preparing a new charge, the gunnery sergeant beginning to bark his orders. I realized then that the artillery observer could not see Red Eagle for the bend in the bluff.

Scrambling from the dugout, I broke through the screen of pines. I fired the Winchester skyward, watched the battery commander searching for the source of the report. He lifted one hand to screen his eyes against the snow glare. I waved the Winchester. "Hold fire!" I shouted. "Truce party!"

When I was satisfied that the batterymen understood, I turned back to Marisa. She was outside the dugout.

"Red Eagle—" I began.

"I saw him," she said hopelessly.

I led her back over the ridge to my horse. The roan was reluctant to take a double mount, but after some persuasion we managed it. We rode back down to the flat ground along the creek, following Red Eagle out toward the gun emplacement. Colonel Comstock was mounted in front of B Troop, waiting.

By the time Marisa and I reached the twelve-pounder, a cluster of batterymen was gathered around Comstock and Red Eagle. The chief was still holding the white cloth upright on his ramrod. "Red Eagle has come to tell the soldier chief what is in his heart," he said. "The Cheyenne are tired of running and fighting. It is cold and we have few blankets. There is nothing to eat. Red Eagle's people can fight no more."

Before the colonel could reply, a sudden flurry of movement broke around the outside of the circle, and a horseman pushed his way into the center. It was Sardis Pender, his thick lips breaking into a broad grin. He edged his mount in beside Colonel Comstock.

I wondered how far back in the rear Pender had been during the skirmishing.

He laughed that little high-pitched snicker of his, and said: "We caught you again, Red Eagle, and this time we'll put you in chains and keep you there."

Red Eagle's face showed pure hatred. He drew his shoulders back, his eyes enlarging as he glared at Pender. At last he turned toward Comstock. "Red Eagle promised surrender only to the soldier chief. The Cheyenne will die before they become prisoners of the agent Pender!"

Comstock glanced sharply at Pender, then replied calmly to Red Eagle: "If your people will come out and give up their arms, I will spare their lives."

Red Eagle bowed his head. "What use are our lives if we must go back under this bad white agent?" he cried.

Pender forced his horse in closer to the chief. "If I had my way, I'd string you to the nearest tree, you yeller-livered lyin' bastard!"

"Mr. Pender!" Comstock interrupted harshly. "I must ask you to leave off interfering in this matter." He turned to the Cheyenne chief. "Your people will become prisoners of the United States Army, to be fed and cared for and protected until you are returned to a reservation. That is all that I, a soldier chief, can promise."

Red Eagle's face was inscrutable. Then his head bowed forward as he spoke. "Red Eagle has heard what is in the soldier chief's heart. Now let the soldier chief order a rifle fired three times. This will tell my people to come out and surrender."

Watching a people surrender is not a pretty way to spend an afternoon. I'd been through that before, on the loser's side at Vicksburg, when we laid down our arms to the Yankees. Seeing a surrender from the conqueror's side that day in the frozen hills above the Yellowhorse didn't leave the act any less bitter to my taste.

I rode in with the burial party to find what might be left of Peter Dunreath. We passed a broken file of women and children in rags, more than a hundred of them, and then the beaten-looking, bandaged warriors, remnants of the once-proud defenders of the tribe, riding their horses slowly up the creek.

I climbed the icy bluffs with the first platoon and saw the results of the exploded shells—twisted bodies, all women and children, half buried under earth and rocks and debris. I helped the men gather up some ragged blankets and robes to wrap the dead and then went on into the woods toward Red Eagle's abandoned tee-pee.

Dunreath saw me before I saw him, and he came leaping toward me through the snow like a startled deer. He was barefooted and wild-eyed and was taking long steps over the snow. "Be damned!" he cried. "Thought you'd never get here, Singleterry, boy!"

"My plans didn't jibe with the colonel's," I said. "Where're your boots?"

"Chee-roo, boy, when I heard that first big shell come a-whishin' through the trees, I lit out for the next coulee. I reckon that Injun guard was hidin' his head; anyway, he didn't try for me."

"Let's fetch your boots and get out of here. It's all over but the big bamboozle."

On the way back to the battalion's position, I told Dunreath something of what had happened—Sardis Pender's unexpected appearance, Colonel Comstock's unusual behavior in the agent's presence, my forced stay in the headquarters tent. "Looks to me as if Pender's got a burr under the colonel's tail," I said, "and I don't look for any easy time around the Twelfth Cavalry while the agent's with us."

A sort of commissary post had been established on a level space beside the creek. The pack mules were brought forward, rations unloaded, cooking fires started, and the creek's ice broken to procure water for boiling coffee. Comstock was sitting on a log near one of the fires. He had covered his ears with a woolen scarf and was idly rubbing snow over his frostbitten cheeks. He looked sick to death, his skin a peculiar gray. Beyond him, the Cheyennes had been herded into a circle ringed with armed troopers, and Pender was swaggering around in his long-tailed coat, taunting the captured warriors.

When Comstock saw Dunreath with me, he got up slowly from the log. "I'm grateful to see that you escaped harm, Pete. Jack Singleterry was not so confident as I that you would wriggle out of this alive."

"Luck, sir, luck," Dunreath replied. "For thirty years I been plain lucky."

"I trust your luck will hold at least until you've scouted us back to Goldfield. Nearly three hundred extra mouths to feed"—he waved back at the captured Cheyennes—"scarcely two days' rations for the troops, and not enough game in these hills to feed a scarecrow. What about that short route to Goldfield you spoke about a while back?"

Dunreath squinted at the hazy sun for a minute, then nodded. "Wouldn't be easy," he drawled. "But we could shave a day or two, mebbe."

I left them there on the log and went to the circle of armed troopers. The keening of mourning squaws rose over the sounds of horses in motion around the temporary bivouac. I searched until I found Marisa. She was with Medicine Woman, both of them huddled together for warmth. The old squaw had pulled her matted hair down over her face. I pushed through the circle and walked over to them. I took out all the hardtack and dried beef that I had in my oilcloth pocket pouch and handed the food to the girl. She looked at me as if she wished me dead, but she took the hardtack and beef and gave some of it to the old woman.

A big, heavy hand clamped down on my shoulder, and I knew it was Pender before he snickered. "Pick 'em purty, don't you, Mr. Singleterry? I used to call this one Little Blue Eyes, a real genuine female hellcat. Half-breed. You never can tell what a she half-breed'll do, Singleterry. Might love you to death one minute, stick a knife in your back the next."

I brushed Pender's hand off my shoulder.

He drew away from me, his thick lips grinning under his curving mustache. "Real rebel, ain't you, mister? Secesh in the late war, they tell me."

"That's right," I said. "And if I thought you had guts enough to be a Yankee soldier, I'd be in favor of starting that little old war going again right here."

Instead of returning to Goldfield over the route we had come, Colonel Comstock decided to take the short way over the mountains to the Yellowhorse River, although Peter Dunreath warned him it would be a rough journey with deep snow on the range and a sharp two-thousand-foot drop to the river.

I remember Comstock asking him: "What sort of trail goes down that drop?"

"Goat path," Dunreath replied. "Zigzag and narrow. The howitzer will have to be dismounted and roped down. Our prisoners will have to drag their travois by hand. Mules with full packs might not make all the turns."

"Could we manage the descent in half a day?"

Dunreath nodded. "And for them that's careless, in less'n half a minute."

It was shortage of horses and rations that led Comstock to choose the more difficult passage. He hoped to save two days' marching that way. With all the warriors and half the women on foot, it was impossible to move rapidly over any route. He figured we'd be better off going slow over a short route than going slow over a long route.

Dunreath and I left camp before dawn—the day following Red Eagle's surrender—and we worked out a march route to the base of a flat-topped range that lay between us and the river. At the mouth of a canyon, I turned back to pick up the column's point, while Dunreath went on up the slope.

By the time I sighted the first patrols, the morning was well along, but a hazy sky screened out what little warmth there was in the sun. I signaled the patrols to turn the point leftward so as to bring the column into direct line with the canyon pass. Holding the roan to a slow canter, I watched the column turn until I could see the whole line of march strung out across the rolling snow field. The Cheyennes were bunched behind the first troop, the column slowed down to the speed of the walking captives.

The Cheyennes had less than forty horses and the battalion only about twenty spare mounts. Upon these horses the women captives were mounted double, with attached travois dragging the children, piles of ragged blankets, and other gear. Several women were walking behind the horses with the warriors.

As I came up to the side of the column, I could hear the travois scraping over the crusted snow. I saw Medicine Woman riding with another squaw, but Marisa was not with the riders. She was walking with Red Eagle and the warriors, a few paces behind the chief, swinging her arms like a soldier. Around her moccasins she had wrapped strips of blanket.

She couldn't avoid seeing me as I rode in close; she glanced briefly at me, her eyes giving me that blue flash of hatred, then she looked away proudly.

I rode quickly on to the front to report to Colonel Comstock.

We stopped for nooning at the mouth of the canyon, and while we were eating our short ration of hardtack and cold salt pork, Peter Dunreath returned. "We can make it to the summit, all right," he informed the colonel. "Snow's deeper up there but no crust."

That afternoon we got our first taste of the rugged passage. The canyon route was so steep in places, troopers had to be sent back to help pull the pack mules along. To save the underfed horses, Comstock ordered everyone to dismount, including the Cheyenne women.

I remember passing through a patch of burned-over timber, the black trunks standing tall and stark like skeletons against the snow; then suddenly almost at duskfall the point riders reached the summit. We burst up out of the shadowy rocks onto a pine-studded level with a two-thousand-foot precipice directly below us. The view was startling, with ruddy sunlight on a rocky range that faced us across the valley of the Yellowhorse.

We bivouacked there on the edge of the precipice, the sun setting before we finished picketing and hobbling mounts. We raced the darkness, cutting pine boughs to pile over the snow for beds. On Comstock's orders we were held to a ration of one cup of sugarless coffee and a thin strip of dried army beef.

Remembering that I had a broken pack of hardtack in my saddlebag, I took half of it and walked through the Indians' camp until I found Marisa. She was sitting cross-legged, watching the flames of her night fire.

"Hello," I said, kneeling down beside her.

She barely glanced at me and looked away, proud and angry. I dropped the hardtack in the lap of her blanket skirt. She ignored the gift, her chin lifting a little.

A familiar sound broke from across the fire: "Huh-huh-he—"

Jerking my head up, I saw Sardis Pender's big body rising from the shadows beyond the fire. He cut his laughter off, and his high voice whined out across the cold, echoing air. "Hardtack won't get you no place hardly at all, Singleterry. Sugar candy now, that's different. Give Little Blue Eyes some sugar candy, and I bet you can't keep her out of your—"

I started walking around the fire toward him, and I suppose the firelight on my face must have told him how angry I was. Oh, I was young and full of spirit in those days, and my feelings had been rubbed raw enough in Pender's presence during the past two days to set me spoiling for a fight. He would have had one, too, but he backed down like the bushwacker he was, stepping away from me and whining. "Didn't mean nothing personal, Mr. Singleterry. Just passing the time with a friendly remark."

I walked on past him, angry at myself for letting him get under my skin. I went on to the fire, where Peter Dunreath and I had spread pine boughs for our blankets. Dunreath was already asleep. I lay back against my saddle, looking out across that deep black precipice, watching the stars sparkle until a young moon came out. In the moonlight the inaccessible gray peaks looked close enough to touch with an outstretched hand, and I thought of Marisa, as unreachable as those mountains, and I wondered if I could ever make that little golden-skinned hostile believe I was her friend.

When I began to drowse, a sensation of guilt jogged keenly at my conscience, and I remembered that before the battalion left Fort Lincoln I had promised Beth Comstock to think of her every night before I fell asleep.

Next morning Dunreath and I were out early, searching a passage through the snow to the drop-off trail. We soon discovered there was no easy route. Snow was piled two or three feet deep along the lee slope, soft and yielding as feathers. The column would have to cross more than a mile of the stuff before we could begin the descent. As far as we could determine, the down trail itself, however, had been swept fairly clean by winds.

When we finally reached the rock cut that marked the beginning of the descending trail, Dunreath fired off his rifle as a signal to Comstock that we had made it through. We waited until the head of the column came up, then started down that devil's pathway. I wouldn't have bet a row of pins on the column's chances to make the descent without serious accident. Fear of high places never bothered me, but I'd sooner walk barefooted over hot coals than make that journey under the same conditions again. It was impossible to stay mounted; we finally gave over to leading our horses all the way, and my roan resisted every one of those treacherous turns.

Miraculously, we had only one accident. A flash of shadow, like that of a great bird, pulled me up short; my eyes focused on the falling object an instant before it vanished—a pack mule spinning to its death. It struck a sharp rock somewhere below with a sound like ripping canvas.

We went downward more and more slowly, until we could see the coffee-colored Yellowhorse flowing below us. Far down the stream was a flat stretch of sunlit green where the snow had all melted.

Sometime around midafternoon we were fording the ice-filled river above a rapids, the lead troop filing onto the stretch of greening grass. This was the first trace of fresh grass our horses had seen in months, and it was hard to hold them.

Colonel Comstock ordered cooking fires lighted for boiling what coffee the commissary had left and then he summoned officers and scouts for a council. After taking a report from the commissary lieutenant on the state of our rations, he asked Dunreath to estimate the distance and likely condition of the route into Goldfield. Dunreath figured it would take eighteen hours slow-marching. "Put all them squaw Cheyenne and young boys on your cavalry mounts, Colonel, we might make it in fourteen."

"And turn my troopers into foot soldiers?"

Dunreath squinted at the sky above the canyon wall. "Fixin' to rain in another day, Colonel. Your troopers can walk twice as fast as them starved squaws and little boys. If rain or more snow catches us, Colonel, sir, you goin' to have a bunch of sick Injuns to bother with."

Comstock rubbed his eyes wearily. "I'll consider your suggestion, Mr. Dunreath," he said, and turned to the commissary officer. "Ration out enough of that salt pork, Lieutenant, to make up a soup for the captives. Mules relieved of ration packs will be slaughtered. And I want two details sent out in opposite directions along the riverbank to hunt game. In here the chances aren't good, but we'll make a try."

By nightfall the temperature dropped back to freezing, and that long slope of greening grass, so attractive by daylight, proved a poor bivouac site after dark. Beneath the short grass the earth was damp from melted snow, and even with a poncho between my blankets and the ground I could feel the raw chill rising. As our only source of fuel was a scanty supply of driftwood along the riverbank, fires were few and small.

I tried in vain to sleep, finally sat up in disgust with my blanket around my shoulders, and began poking at the dying fire. "This is a good night for a dirty detail like sentry duty," I said to Dunreath, who was curled up on the other side. "Since a man can't sleep anyhow, he'd be better off keeping warm walking post."

Dunreath grunted. I knew he'd be asleep in another minute; Dunreath could have slept on the cold muddy bottom of the Missouri River.

The moon wasn't up yet, and cloud scud partially obscured the stars. The Yellowhorse, full of ice chunks, rushed noisily along under the night. *That water has a long way to go,* I thought, *all the way down to the Gulf of Mexico and the warm lazy country where I wish I was.*

I was just reaching out my hands to warm them over the little rising flame when I heard a whispering motion in the frosted grass behind me. Thinking one of our horses had broken a hobble and strayed, I got up and started toward the animals. A whimpering sound brought me up short. At first I thought it might be a young animal lost in the night, then a choked-off sob told me it came from a human being.

As my eyes grew accustomed to the darkness, I could see a dark shape against the grass. I took a step forward and kneeled down, my fingers touching braided hair, and then a face came up out of the blanket.

"Marisa!" I whispered.

She started to say something, but another sob broke over her words. She was shivering under the blanket. I lifted her to her feet and led her over toward the fire.

In the darkness I could see only her eyes gleaming fearfully at me. She resisted, shaking her head. "You're freezing," I said, urging her closer to the fire. With my boot I dragged my saddle in closer and motioned her to sit down.

Dunreath was snoring in his blankets. She glanced at him and then sat on the saddle, squeezing her blanketed knees together with her arms, bending her head and shoulders forward like a scolded, frightened child. I moved away from her, watching her, waiting for her to talk.

But she wasn't going to talk. "You're afraid of something," I said. "Tell me what it is and the fear will go away."

She shook her head and one of her braids slipped loose and dropped over the outside of the blanket. Her teeth were clenched over her bottom lip.

"You can trust me," I said.

She turned her head and looked straight at me. "Marisa will never trust a man who wears white skin," she said.

"After what's happened to you, I don't blame you," I replied.

She relaxed just a little. "You are a strange one, soldier scout. You led the bluecoats and their big-talking gun to our hiding place so they could kill women and children, but you have been kind to Marisa. No one else has been kind to Marisa. I see the eyes of the other white men watching me, but there is no kindness in their looks. They are all like the one called Pender."

"What about Pender?" I asked.

"He came to me tonight," she said with cold hatred. "He came prancing about like a great male bear and ordered Medicine Woman to go to the other side of the Cheyenne encampment, and then—"

I moved closer to her. "Where is Pender now?"

She put her head down, shaking it from side to side.

"I'll find him," I said, and turned to go.

THE OLD-TIMERS

These two grizzled knights of the Old West never listen when folks say they're over the hill—they just use their true grit, their know-how, and a little luck to tame even the meanest young outlaws.

☐ **THE OLD-TIMERS OF GUN SHY**
16565-2 $2.95

☐ **THE OLD-TIMERS IN THE SANGRE DE CRISTOS**
20032-6 $2.95

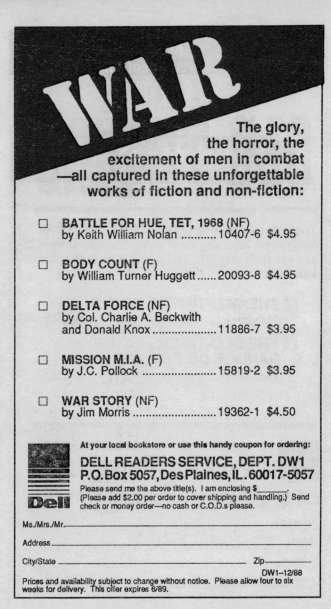

Special Offer
Buy a Dell Book
For only 50¢.

Now you can have Dell's Readers Service Listing filled with hundreds of titles. Plus, take advantage of our unique and exciting bonus book offer which gives you the opportunity to purchase a Dell book for *only 50¢.* Here's how!

Just order any five books at the regular price. Then choose any other single book listed (up to $5.95 value) for just 50¢. Use the coupon below to send for Dell's Readers Service Listing of titles today!

DELL READERS SERVICE LISTING
P.O. Box 1045, South Holland, IL. 60473

Ms./Mrs./Mr. _____

Address _____

City/State _____ Zip _____

DFCA -12/88